D0457711

Guilty Confections

Karen Kelly

Annie's®

AnniesFiction.com

Library of Congress-in-Publication Data
Guilty Confections / by Karen Kelly
p. cm.
I. Title
2016952132

AnniesFiction.com
(800) 282-6643
Chocolate Shoppe Mysteries™
Series Creator: Shari Lohner
Series Editors: Janice Tate, Ken Tate
Cover Illustrator: Bonnie Leick

Dead? she thought. *Two young brothers caught up in the rancor of the coming Civil War, and one killed the other right here at Belle Haven!*

Jillian Green's weapons of warfare stood at attention on the pristinely scrubbed butcher block counter of her grandmother's kitchen. She touched each one as she read aloud from her laptop computer. "Brown sugar, raisins, butter, vanilla, water, more butter, white sugar, baking powder, milk, flour. One Idiot's Delight cake coming right up."

Jillian gave a determined nod, her dark-red ponytail bobbing against her neck. If she could successfully make this recipe, named for its simplicity, maybe she could one day take over The Chocolate Shoppe Bakery for her grandmother—whom she called by her first name, Bertie—without burning it down. Since returning to Moss Hollow from California a few months before, she'd become a fair hand at cupcake and cookie decoration. But baking them in the massive professional ovens had not been as simple. Jillian figured she'd practice with the less imposing oven at Belle Haven, her family's ancestral home, and work her way up.

With her favorite songs ringing out from her digital music player, Jillian placed a saucepan, hefty enough to be used as self-defense, on the stove and turned the temperature dial to medium. After dropping the brown sugar, raisins, pat of butter, vanilla, and four cups of water into the pan, she grabbed a wooden spoon from the utensil drawer and stirred the ingredients in time with the music until everything was melted and mixed.

Then, sucking in a deep breath, she turned the heat higher. Concentrate, Jillian. Don't blow it on the first skirmish. She'd purposely picked a time for her experiment when she knew both Bertie and her great-aunt Cornelia would be away from the rambling old plantation house for a couple of hours. But if she left behind the stench of burnt sugar and raisins, she'd have to answer for it.

She'd rather kiss a gator.

"The batter!" Squinting at the recipe again, Jillian realized she probably should have made the batter first. Why didn't they put that in the instructions? The authors of the recipe obviously overestimated the baking prowess of some cooks. She turned the heat way down so the sauce mixture would be safe from burning and dumped the rest of the ingredients into a mixing bowl attached to the standing mixer that was almost as intimidating as Bertie when her dander was up. "Oh no. What if the sauce gets too cool and thickens too much?" Up the heat went again, but not as high as before. Chewing the inside of her lip, Jillian bounced her attention between the batter and the sauce, hoping she hadn't already bungled it by not thinking ahead. That was a trait that had complicated her life a few times in her almost four decades, and those complications had recently led her back to her childhood home after twenty years away.

But, truthfully, Jillian was almost at the point of enjoying the changes in her life, not simply accepting them. *Well, except the whole training-to-be-a-master-chef thing.* That was going to take longer.

The mixer had pummeled the simple ingredients into a thick batter. Jillian switched off the power and tilted the body of the mixer away from the bowl, scraping the clinging globs from the beaters. After dropping spoonfuls of batter into a pan she'd greased, Jillian poured the sweet sauce from the stove over them. Now came the scary part, the part she tended to mess up. She lowered the door of the oven and slid the pan into the center. Double-checking the time in the recipe, she set the timer on her phone, poured herself a glass of sweet tea, and padded out to the veranda. She gazed out over the front garden that Aunt Cornelia had brought back to life since she'd moved in with her twin sister, a move precipitated by the death of Cornelia's husband, Raymond. She might be in her late seventies, but Jillian wouldn't be surprised if she could coax a beautiful bloom from a sandbur.

The swing gave a muffled squeak when Jillian sat down, but it was solid beneath her as she tucked her legs under her and leaned back. It was the last day of September and just about as hot as it had been in August. Only a friendly breeze and the ice-cold glass in hand kept her from escaping back inside to the air-conditioned house. Soon, lulled by the gentle movement of the swing, Jillian's eyes started to close.

A mass of creamy white fur thumped onto her lap and began jabbing her stomach in rhythm. "Oof! Possum, stop! It's too hot for a cat lap blanket." The cat turned blue eyes her way, pranced like a vineyard girl stomping grapes for another ten seconds, and then launched himself onto the veranda floor and over the banister. "Silly cat," Jillian mumbled as she closed her eyes again.

Jillian jerked awake at the smell of something burning. "Wha—? My Idiot's Delight!" She ran into the kitchen as a haze of smoke was beginning to fill the spacious room. "No! No! No!" Grabbing pot holders from their hooks on the wall by the stove, she opened the oven door, coughing as a thicker smoke billowed into her face. She stepped back, took a deep breath, and held it before plunging her hands into the oven to pull out the Idiot's Delight cake, which was looking far from delightful.

Shoving the pan into the sink, Jillian returned to the oven to turn it off, chastising herself. "How did this happen? You even set an alarm!" She pulled her phone from the pocket of her shorts and peered at it through the gray haze. The alarm showed two options, cancel and resume. Possum must have knocked it into pause mode when he was kneading her like bread dough. Or maybe it's just someone trying to tell me that I'm not cut out to be a baker. She groaned as she examined the charred remains of the dessert that she had planned to serve Bertie and Cornelia after dinner. The sweet sauce had pretty much burned up, leaving what looked like glazed hockey pucks. Some of the folks of Moss Hollow would probably be happy to use them for target practice.

Out of the corner of her eye, Jillian saw movement at the kitchen door. Possum poked his head up into the haze, his nose twitching. "Don't even think about it." Jillian shook a finger at the cat. "You've done quite enough damage for one day."

The cat sneezed and left.

After prying as much of the dessert from the pan as she could with knife and spatula, Jillian filled the pan with hot soapy water and left it to soak. There was no hiding her disaster from her family now. Sure, she could blame it on Possum, but a part of her suspected she would have ruined the dessert even without his help. Escaping the smelly kitchen, she went back to the veranda and called her childhood friend, Savannah Cantrell.

"Hi, Jillian. What's up?"

With Savannah's kind voice in her ear, Jillian hesitated to dump her problems on her friend. After all, they'd only reconnected a few months ago. "Not much. Am I interrupting anything?" Savannah had a bookkeeping business and stayed busy, even in the small town of Moss Hollow.

"No, I'm pretty much done for the week. You know not much work gets done on Friday afternoons around here. Especially during hunting season." Her friend paused. "So, what's wrong? Is everyone all right?"

Jillian puffed out her cheeks. "Am I that obvious?"

"Well, maybe not to everyone," Savannah consoled her, "but even when we were kids I could tell."

"You and Bertie." She sighed and told her friend the sad tale of the charred Idiot's Delight cake. "Savannah, how am I going to keep The Chocolate Shoppe going if I'm not able to bake anything edible on a consistent basis?" Her forehead dropped onto her raised knee. "I don't want to let Bertie down."

"You're not letting anyone down. You simply need to learn a new skill, that's all. Bertie's been baking since antiquity, and you've just started." Jillian heard a soft chuckle. "Remember how in high school I knew I'd fly through college for accounting and graduate with honors?"

"I remember how much I teased you about it."

"Well, you went off to college in California, so you never knew that I almost flunked my first accounting classes. They were so much harder than I had expected. I'd call my mom and cry in her ear every week for the first couple of semesters."

"Really?" Jillian tried to picture her friend like that and found it a stretch. "But half the businesses in town rely on you, for good reason."

"Now. They would have steered clear like I was wearing eau de skunk perfume if they'd seen me my freshman year. And that's my point. I struggled to learn what I needed but eventually mastered those skills and created a solid business. You can do this."

Jillian's next words came in a whisper. "I sure hope you're right."

"I'm coming over. Pour me some tea."

The call ended, leaving Jillian staring at her phone. Even after years of separation and misunderstanding in their past, Savannah had shown herself to be a better friend than all the people she'd known in California as a successful marketing executive. They'd disappeared much faster than the smoke in Bertie's kitchen as soon as she'd lost her position, another victim of her fiancé's plunge into white-collar crime.

By the time Savannah climbed the steps of the veranda, a tall glass of tea awaited her.

"Drink up." Jillian waved her friend over to a porch chair next to a wicker side table. "You're going to need the sugar jolt."

Savannah raised her sunglasses to stare at her. "What I need is the best sweet tea in the county, and your family makes it." She raised the frosty glass in a salute and took a long drink.

"Not the whole family. Bertie and Cornelia. I'm a little rusty."

Savannah shook her head as she lowered the glass. "You've been out of practice for two decades, Jillian. Give yourself some slack. Don't let one little mishap steal your confidence."

"It hasn't stolen my confidence. But I'm a realistic person, and the truth is I'm not sure I've got what it takes to keep The Chocolate Shoppe Bakery afloat and help Bertie and Aunt Cornelia."

Savannah's thin fingers cradled the glass. "Now, I know that's not true. So it might take some time and work to learn the finer points of baking." She raised a finger as Jillian opened her mouth. "Let me finish." Jillian squinted but kept silent. "Until then, there are plenty of ways you can help." She pulled her smartphone from her purse. "I have a notebook app that I use all the time. We can make a list."

"You and your list making." Jillian smiled in spite of herself.

"Nothing like a good brainstorming session. Right, Ms. Marketing?"

Jillian shrugged but didn't argue.

Savannah exchanged her sunglasses for her usual wire-framed pair of glasses and began coaxing Jillian into admitting as many of her abilities as she could think of. When Jillian was beginning to think her head would explode, Savannah signaled that the list was completed. "Now, we just need to pick one place to start helping."

"I know exactly where Jillian should start." The two friends startled at the voice from the door behind them.

Cornelia's brimmed hat and comfortable clothes signaled she was headed out to work in the gardens. "How long have you been there, Aunt Cornelia?" It surprised Jillian that neither she nor Savannah had heard her aunt's classic powder-blue mustang arrive home.

"Long enough. But I knew you would need direction today anyway." Possum rubbed against her ankles.

Oh no, not again. But she had to ask. "How?"

"The haint told me in a dream last night. I didn't know what she meant until just now when I heard you two talking."

"The haint?" Savannah asked politely, throwing a glance Jillian's way.

"Yes, dear. The haint of Belle Haven, Virginia Belle," Aunt Cornelia said with a smile, as though Virginia were a cousin she lunched with on a regular basis instead of the dead wife of Captain Hoyt Belle, who had built the mansion two hundred years ago.

At least this time, she said she had dreamed the conversation, rather than having a purported face-to-face chat with the ghost rumored to still be in residence in the home. That was about as normal as Jillian could hope for when it came to her eccentric aunt. "So where do you think I should start, Aunt Cornelia?"

"Not me, dear. The haint. She was very adamant, so there must be a good reason she said what she said. It will probably help us all."

"Okay, I'll bite. What did 'the haint' say?"

"She said the answer is in the attic." Her aunt's blue eyes sparkled as though she'd just saved Jillian from a lifetime of futility.

The attic. The attic that probably hadn't been touched in fifty years and surely contained enough dust to stuff a dozen mattresses. Jillian glanced Savannah's way. That was a lot to ask, even from a childhood friend. "Aunt Cornelia, I'll see what I can do—I mean, find—in the attic after Savannah and I have finished."

"Nonsense," said Savannah. "I'd love to poke around up there. It's such a cool old place."

Jillian snorted. "On the contrary. It's a hot, stuffy place this time of year. But if you insist, I won't stop you. We'd better carry up a gallon of tea, though."

"I just made a new batch, so make sure you take the chilled one," Aunt Cornelia said. Jillian expected her to mention the lingering smell of smoke, but she didn't. "Happy hunting." She disappeared back inside the house, but shortly afterward, Jillian and Savannah saw her striding through the grass of the front lawn toward a flower bed, gardening tools in hand.

Soon, the two women were climbing the sweeping center staircase with their own tools: brooms, dusters, bags, and enough microfiber cloths to stock any respectable Piggly Wiggly grocery store. A wave of stale, hot air hit them when Jillian opened the third floor attic door. "Ugh." Jillian instinctively stepped back. "And I thought the kitchen was hot."

"We have to open those windows." Savannah eyed the jumble of possessions between them and fresh air. "If we can get to them."

Jillian moved to her left, peering around a large spinning wheel that listed sideways. "I think we can move most of the stuff to reach that one at least." She grabbed what looked like safe places on the old wheel and lifted it off the floor to scoot it aside enough to form the beginning of a path. It wasn't long before they reached the dormer window. "If this doesn't open, I'm done."

Savannah squeezed beside her. "On three, push your side. One, two, three."

The window shuddered and groaned as the two women strained against the years of nonuse. At last it began to inch upward. Once they had raised it as high as it would go, they propped the attic door open to create airflow and went to work.

Jillian was astounded at the collection of antiques and curios gathered under the eaves. "I know Bertie would be horrified at the thought of selling off part of Belle Haven's past, but people would pay some serious cash for a lot of these things." She pulled a fat photo album from a bookcase, wiped off the thick layer of dust, and opened it. "Look at this. It's filled with old postcards."

Savannah looked over her shoulder. "I know someone who makes good money buying cards like these at auctions and reselling them online. It never would have occurred to me, but she's sold some for a couple hundred dollars each."

"Wow. I was thinking more of the furniture and curios, but postcards would be much easier to ship." Jillian carefully placed the album back on the dusted shelf. "I wonder what Cornelia had in mind. 'The answer is in the attic.' Do you see an answer?"

"Not yet. But whatever it is, it's bound to be interesting." Savannah poked the broom under a pine cupboard. A couple of marbles rolled toward her foot. She scooped them into her hand and held them up to the afternoon light streaming through the windows. "These are beauties. Made when each marble was different, instead of mass produced."

They worked, dusting and straightening, through the afternoon. Eventually, probably from dust-induced insanity, Jillian broached the subject of where to start in tackling the new baking techniques she needed. "Is there a remedial class for those who have flopped at even Idiot's Delight cakes?"

"You know the Sweetie Pies would be happy to help you, Jillian," Savannah said. "It'll be a nice . . . a change of pace from the usual—"

Crash!

Savannah's words were cut off as a mahogany vanity table toppled over, striking a mottled mirror and shattering it to bits.

The two friends stared at each other, catching their breath. "What was that?" Savannah asked, pulling a three-legged stool from a corner and dropping onto it.

"I didn't get a good look, but I thought I glimpsed a ball of fluff streaking out the door," Jillian said.

"You think it was Possum? Your cat can wreak that much havoc?"

"He's not my cat," Jillian retorted. "But yeah. It had to be Possum, friend to cardiac specialists everywhere." She blew out a deep breath, trying to remember what she'd learned about restorative breathing from the lone yoga class she'd taken in California. She knew she'd really had a fright when such a random part of her past entered her mind. As soon as the teacher had started talking about "balancing her chi," she'd decided she'd stick to humor for stress management. "Well, at least the millions of tiny shards we have to clean up aren't dusty anymore."

Savannah gave her a wan smile. "That makes me feel so much better."

After a few minutes of rest, Jillian examined the fallen vanity table. "I think the legs are okay. Help me lift this."

"Sure." Together, the friends raised the side of the table. Before it came upright, a drawer fell open and something thudded onto the wide-planked floor.

Jillian leaned over the corner of the table and retrieved the object. It was a wraparound leather-bound book with a tarnished lock. "Looks like a journal. A really old one." She fingered the lock, but it wouldn't open. "Is there a key still in the drawer?"

Savannah peered into the wide, shallow drawer, then reached

a hand inside. "No." They searched the area nearby. "If we can't find it, maybe we can figure out a way to pick it. You can find instruction videos for anything online."

There was a delay in Jillian's response as she crouched beside a knothole in the floor. She crowed in triumph. "That won't be necessary." She stood up, holding a small but sturdy skeleton key. Inserting it into the diary's lock, she gently turned. When it didn't move, she changed the angle of the key and tried again. With a muffled click, the lock scraped opened.

"I feel like a character in a kid's mystery novel," Savannah whispered.

Jillian cradled the book in her left hand and carefully freed the leather flap, which fell open against her wrist, surprising her with its weight. On the first page, the words *The Diary of Bridgett Summerlin* were written in faded ink with a neat hand and flourishes on the initial letter of each word. Underneath was a date—*25 December 1860*—with the notation that the journal was a gift made by her dear brother, Charles.

"Wow, it's in great shape for being more than 150 years old," Savannah said, her voice still a whisper.

Jillian nudged her friend. "It's lasted this long. I think you can speak in your usual volume without it disintegrating."

A sheepish look crossed Savannah's features. "You got me. I whisper in museums too," she admitted, although in a slightly louder voice. "I know Belle Haven was built even longer ago, but it's the small details of life that grab me for some reason."

"Thanks for the warning, in case we run across some old bedroom slippers and you get the vapors." Jillian turned to the next page and read the first entry aloud.

Perhaps it would have been prudent to wait until the New Year to begin this journal. But I have never been

*able to wait to walk in freshly fallen snow either, much
to Mother's chagrin.*

"Snow? Just how much snow did they get here back then?
Unless frost is the new snow." Savannah bent over the journal.
Jillian continued reading.

> *As I will be traveling soon to visit Aunt Olive and
> Uncle Vernon in Moss Hollow, I want to show Charles
> how much I treasure the gift he made before I leave. The
> lock is particularly fine work. I will miss my family and
> my beloved mountains of Tennessee, but anticipate much
> adventure in Georgia.*

She paused. "Moss Hollow must have been a more exciting
place back then, or Bridgett will have been sorely disappointed
in the lack of adventure."

"Well, she lived in the mountains of Tennessee, and a lot of
that area is still remote even today, especially in winter. Moss
Hollow might have been almost cosmopolitan in comparison."

Jillian chuckled. "Moss Hollow and cosmopolitan, two things
I never thought I'd hear in conjunction with each other." She
skipped ahead several entries. "Oh, she's here now."

> *Belle Haven is the grandest home I've ever visited.
> When I descend the sweeping staircase from my room
> on the second floor and the stained glass dome scatters
> rainbows of light around me, I feel like a princess.*

"I wonder which room she was given."

"Have you ever felt like a princess here?" Savannah asked.

Jillian thought about it. "I remember sneaking into Bertie's closet when I was about five and wearing one of her summer nighties like a ball gown. It was all fun and light until I tripped on the hem and descended three quarters of the stairs head over heels. I've had a healthy respect, rather than fancy, for that staircase ever since."

"Ouch. Sorry I asked." Savannah nodded at the journal. "What else does Bridgett write about?"

Jillian scanned through several entries. "Buggy rides, church meetings, large dinners, needlework, music, and cooking. She wrote down some recipes she learned from her aunt's kitchen. See? Everyone in my family tree can bake except me."

"Given the year and the fact that Belle Haven was a working plantation, Aunt Olive probably did more managing than baking, I would think. What kinds of recipes?"

"Cream of celery soup, Roman punch, chicken fricassee." Turning some more pages, Jillian scanned another entry and tapped Savannah on the arm. "Here, like this dinner party she went to for some other out-of-towners. Look at the menu for one meal." She stepped back to give her friend room.

Savannah bent over the old book, murmuring as she read. "Some of Moss Hollow's restaurants have shorter menus. I'm sure there were several cooks for all that food." She touched a finger down on a page. "Bridgett writes here about the guests of honor, Amherst and Cyrena Stone. Those names sound familiar, but I just can't place *why*. I'm going to do some research tonight." She brushed a smudge of dirt off her arm. "After a nice long bath."

Jillian realized the shadows were gaining ground in the attic. "Let's call it a day. We actually accomplished a lot, and I don't trust the electrical wiring up here enough to stay after dark. If this imaginary haint wants me to do more, she's going to have to be more specific in Cornelia's dreams."

The women gathered up their cleaning supplies and Bridgett's journal, checked to make sure they weren't locking Possum in the attic, closed the window, and made their way to the first floor, stopping long enough for Jillian to leave the book in her room. After stowing away the cleaning items, Jillian walked Savannah to her car.

Her friend started the engine, then stuck her head out the window. "Don't forget to tell me about any juicy tidbits you find in the rest of the journal."

"You'll be the first to know," Jillian promised.

As Savannah's car disappeared down the driveway, Jillian gasped. She'd been so occupied with the attic and their discovery that she'd completely forgotten about the charred dessert sitting in the kitchen sink. But when she ran to clean up the mess, the entire space was spotless and the air smelled fresh with not even a lingering hint of smoke. If her grandmother had come home to find her favorite room in the house in such a state, Jillian would probably hear about it sooner rather than later. But after all the work Bertie or Cornelia had done, she could only be thankful that someone had finished the job and wondered how they had neutralized the smell so thoroughly.

After making and devouring a sandwich, she nibbled on a crisp apple from the fridge as she plodded upstairs to draw a relaxing bath in the spacious claw-foot tub in the bathroom on the second floor.

The colorful stained glass dome arching above her head, the same one that had so delighted Bridgett, was now muted in the twilight. Considering how many things around the sprawling plantation house had deteriorated due to age, storm, or human foolishness, Jillian was impressed that the beautiful glass had endured. Just like Belle Haven women had endured, Bertie always insisted.

An hour later, after relaxing in soothing water infused with lavender and bergamot crystals from the beveled glass jar on the antique sink, Jillian ended her bath and settled in for an evening of journal reading. She grabbed her laptop from the desk and created a document to use as a table of contents for Bridgett's journal, to keep track of the recipes and any other interesting information. Glancing at the clock on her computer, Jillian told herself she would only read for a couple of hours since she was scheduled for an early start at The Chocolate Shoppe the next morning. Pretty much everything she did at the bakery took enormous concentration, making sleep a high priority.

As she read on, it became apparent that Bridgett had not been a short-term visitor to Belle Haven, as Jillian read entry after entry about life at her family's home. Having spent more time as a teenager with Bertie than her own parents, Jillian felt a kinship growing for the young woman. At least she had stayed in the same community, unlike Bridgett, who had traveled from Tennessee to live with people she hardly knew in a town she had never seen before in order to attend a young ladies academy and, from what Jillian read, to meet planter-class families. The girl had spirit.

A few months after arriving in Moss Hollow, it sounded like Bridgett had caught the eye of a young man named Jedediah.

Uh-oh. Jillian knew she'd have to keep the journal out of Bertie and Cornelia's sights. They didn't need any additional encouragement to be hunting down a man for her. From what Jillian was reading, the citizens of Moss Hollow had a much longer history of meddling in other people's love lives than she'd realized. Bridgett, however, sounded much less annoyed about it than Jillian was.

I received an invitation to visit the Duprees yesterday.

Mrs. Dupree gave me a tour of the lovely gardens, and Jedediah showed me the peach orchard, his pride and joy. How his eyes lit up when he shared with me his plans for expansion. I hope this will be merely the first of many invitations.

Jillian shook her head at the girl's naïve optimism. *Be careful, girl. He might turn out to be a criminal like my ex-fiancé,* she thought. After her bad experience in love, Jillian's mind and heart had been locked in a tug-of-war, fighting between giving up all hope of ever finding a lifelong partner and throwing herself into a foolhardy plan to meet more single men in the area. Both options terrified her if she thought on them too long. She hoped Bridgett had found an honorable and loving man. Women in those days seldom had many options.

She smiled at an entry about Bridgett's obligation of letter writing. Apparently, writing letters to extended family was the only real chore the young girl had.

I wrote four letters today, one of them to Mother, assuring her that I was indeed conducting myself with the greatest propriety.

The timer Jillian had set to warn her when two hours had passed sounded. She'd have to wait to find out how things had developed for Bridgett and Jedediah.

Rummaging through her nightstand, she found a bookmark and inserted it into the journal. As she began to carefully close the cover, three words popped out at her from the next long entry: *Union soldier* and *bury.* Suddenly feeling more awake, Jillian opened the journal again, telling herself she'd read only one more entry and then turn out the light.

26 March 1861—Jedediah came to Belle Haven this evening, surprising me as I walked in the gardens behind the mansion in the moonlight. The fountains soothe me after the hours of hearing about the possibility of war coming to the South. In the letter from Papa that came today, he wrote that it is not safe for me to travel home now that Georgia has seceded from the Union, and Uncle says he agrees. I have been torn, wanting to stay near Jedediah, but also anxious to know how my parents and brother fare. For now, the decision is out of my hands.

I suggested to Jedediah that it was not strictly appropriate for us to be talking alone. My heart could only sing when he told me he meant no disrespect but was desperate for my opinion on a difficult matter. But, oh! Such a difficult matter. His older brother, Frederick, whom he has always held in the highest esteem, had earlier this evening told him he was firm in his support of the Union. He was even making plans to move his wife, Charlotte, and their child north and fight as a Union soldier if war was to come!

I have never seen this side of Jedediah, so distraught that he tore at his hair and spittle from his lips almost spotted my skirt. I must admit I was at a loss to know what to do. And then, who came through the live oaks but Frederick! He politely acknowledged me before beginning to plead with Jedediah to understand. Jedediah yelled something about how it was Amherst Stone's doing that his brother had become a traitor to his family and state. This confused me, as the Stones seemed a perfectly respectable family, with Mr. Stone being an attorney and businessman in Atlanta, while Mrs. Stone delighted me with her intelligent conversation at the Stansels' dinner. Frederick answered that his decisions were his alone after examining all the facts.

"The facts?" Jedediah yelled, making me wonder if Uncle Vernon would come to investigate. "How about the fact that your decisions will bring disgrace upon our mother and father? Did you consider them at all when you decided to turn into a Northern sympatizer?"

Frederick answered so quietly that I could not hear what he said. But it lit Jedediah up like a lamp oil on fire, and before I could move, he'd swung a mighty blow at his brother. Frederick fell hard, crushing his skull against the fountain. Jedediah didn't have to tell me.

I knew Frederick was dead.

3

Jillian couldn't believe the words she was reading. *Dead?* she thought. *Two young brothers caught up in the rancor of the coming Civil War, and one killed the other right here at Belle Haven?* She had known that the war had split families and had pitted brother against brother, but it had never been so real to her as this moment. Her ancestral home had been the microcosm of that horrific conflict.

The words of the journal again pushed their way into her mind.

Jedediah tried to rouse Frederick, but I knew Frederick was beyond saving. I started to run for help, but Jedediah pleaded with me to stay. He said it would kill his mother to lose both of her sons at the same time. Her heart wasn't strong enough. If we buried Frederick and kept silent, at least Mrs. Dupree would have her youngest son by her side and some time to adjust to the loss of her oldest. He said the family would think that Frederick was headed for Northern soil. Perhaps they would think he had died in battle.

Try as I might to be strong, tears flowed at the thought of the kind lady and her loss. My decision will haunt me all my years, but I agreed to help Jedediah bury Frederick's body on the grounds of Belle Haven beneath a large live oak along the back acreage. Jedediah ran to the tobacco barn for the necessary tools while I sat beside Frederick, shivering at the thought that someone would catch Jedediah. What would I do then?

I almost fainted in relief when he returned with a shovel and hoe. There I was in the dark, hoeing the earth under a tree like a character from one of those Sensation Novels that Mother always warned me about. I'm quite sure she would have been mortified by my actions. Thankfully, I wore gloves or I'm sure the state of my hands would attract notice.

When we were finished, Jedediah took my hand and looked deeply into my eyes. What I saw in his frightened me.

Jillian quickly turned to the next page, eager for more of the story, only to find a description of some dresses her aunt was having made for her. Bridgett was probably still in shock. But she kept skimming from page to page, looking for anything about Jedediah or the Duprees, only to realize Bridgett made no other entries about the horrible event.

Squinting at the clock, Jillian groaned. She had to be up in a few hours to help Lenora Ryan before the shop opened. *How am I going to sleep now?* Tucking the journal into the drawer of her desk, she turned off the light and tried to fall asleep, but questions kept pinging around her brain.

Did Bertie or Aunt Cornelia know about Bridgett and the events of her stay here? Since her aunt loved telling creepy stories, especially to Jillian, surely she would have found some wild, stormy night to freak out her great-niece about a young girl who buried a body in their backyard. Bertie might know, but Jillian would have to pry it out of her, since her focus was solidly fixed on the present state of Belle Haven and The Chocolate Shoppe Bakery. Her grandmother's less-is-more approach with words wouldn't satisfy her curiosity anyway.

Dupree. Jillian only knew one person in Moss Hollow with that name: Otis Dupree, who had been a curmudgeon when she was a little girl and had had twenty more years to perfect his practice. But he lived in a house as old and almost as large as Belle Haven with peach orchards on the property. He was probably the one she should see about Jedediah and Frederick.

She imagined their meeting. "Hello, Mr. Dupree, would you like your ancestor's body back?" Jillian gave a drowsy giggle and finally drifted off to sleep.

When the alarm on her bedside table jolted her awake, she felt like she had been asleep less than a minute, though it was more like three hours. It was little sleep enough for the busy morning shift she had before her. The thought of Bertie's reaction if she was late kept Jillian from rolling over and going back to sleep. Doing a fair impression of a zombie without all the blood and gore, she got up to splash water on her face and get dressed for work before staggering down the stairs to the kitchen.

As she was alternating gulps of coffee with the kind of yawns that prompted people to joke about catching flies, Cornelia danced into the kitchen. "Good morning, Jillian. Did you find your answer in the attic yet?"

Jillian stared into her mug, deciding to wait until she had the chance to talk with Otis Dupree before saying anything to Cornelia or Bertie about the journal. "Not that I can tell. Found a lot of dust and old furniture that might be useful or sellable with a bit of work, and some clothing and portraits. Not an answer in the bunch." She was so tired that she couldn't remember what question she was supposed to be answering.

"Hmmm." Cornelia opened a cupboard and retrieved a mixing bowl. "I'll ask the haint to give me something else to narrow down *where* in the attic you should look." She moved over to the refrigerator, taking out butter and milk. "I'm making some biscuits and gravy. Would you like some?"

Jillian turned bleary eyes to the clock on the stove. She'd been trying to muster the energy to decide what to eat, but her brain only echoed *coffee, coffee, coffee.* "That would be nice, thank you." She was afraid to sit at the table until there was more to occupy her tired mind and body, or she might end up facedown, snoring, so she remained standing, clinging to her mug as if it were a life jacket in a stormy sea. The thought of the fictitious haint giving Cornelia dreams made her a little jealous. *Dreaming takes sleeping, after all.*

Well-fed and with her travel mug by her side, Jillian drove through the darkness with her windows down. Some birds were sounding entirely too cheerful, but she tried to absorb a little of their enthusiasm along with the coolness of the early morning. The first day of October would heat up soon enough, just like the back room of the bakery.

Jillian staggered through the back door into the bright kitchen and saw Lenora look up from her work, dark eyes narrowing. "Girl, you look rough as a cob. If you're sick, you can just turn right around and head for home."

Lenora Ryan, a large-boned African-American woman, was a fixture at The Chocolate Shoppe Bakery. Normally jovial and good-natured, Lenora lived in an apartment above the bakery.

"I'm not sick," Jillian said, almost wishing she were if it would give her a pass to crawl back into bed. "Just a little tired."

"A little, huh?" Lenora handed Jillian a pink hairnet that matched the one covering her own salt-and-pepper hair. "Maybe mixing a little dough will wake you up."

Jillian took one last gulp from her travel mug, stretched her neck from side to side, and drew the netting over her hair. "Okay, let's do this." If Bridgett could bury a body as a teenage girl, she could surely make some bread.

The concentration needed to weigh out the flour, water, salt, and yeast finally brought Jillian out of her fog. She even remembered to use the scale's tare function, something she'd forgotten several times when she'd first started helping at the bakery. Soon, the flour and water were combining—or incorporating, as Bertie had taught her to say—at a medium-slow speed in the workhorse mixer. She had gradually become more comfortable with the language of dough. But the ovens? She'd probably be faster at learning Swahili.

She thought she was doing fine until she stopped the mixer and lifted up the hook, preparing to cover the dough and let it rest. Lenora walked by with a tray of pastries, glancing into the mixer. "Jillian, what are you doing? Can't you see that flour there?" She stabbed the right side of the bowl with her eyes. "Turn the mixer back on again until that flour joins the party." Lenora carried on with her own tasks, shaking her head.

If that had been her only mistake, Jillian would have counted it a successful day. But it wasn't. She overshot the speed during the kneading process, prompting Lenora to remind her that she was baking bread, not cement.

Jillian was wiping down the counter when she heard the expert baker growl. "What now?" she blurted, throwing down the cloth.

"I asked you to make a rustic French loaf, not a sandwich loaf. This has kneaded too long for rustic bread." Lenora flared her nostrils, clasping her hands as though restraining them from throttling Jillian. "Did you forget, or weren't you paying attention?"

Jillian felt a flush heat her already warm face. "I'm sorry. I did listen when you told me, but I lost track of time."

"That's why you set an alarm, like we taught you when you first started learning bread making. It's too easy to get distracted." Lenora stood silently, looking at her until Jillian started fidgeting. Then she waved toward the door. "You best go on home before I lose my temper. Don't come back until you can think straight again."

As Jillian took off her hairnet, she heard Lenora mutter, "I suppose I best be setting a sale on sandwich loaves today." She was so anxious to get out of the kitchen that she found herself scurrying into the front rather than out the back door. As the early-bird customers looked up from their coffees and muffins, she plastered what she hoped was a pleasant look on her face, although she could have looked like a maniacal puppet for all she knew. Pushing open the front door a little harder than usual, she escaped outside . . .

And promptly plowed into Hunter Greyson, the town's handsome mortician. Bracing himself, he reached out to steady Jillian as her momentum caused her to bounce off him. "It's a pleasure to run into you, Jillian." His blue eyes crinkled at the corners, making her feel even worse.

The day just kept getting better.

"Yeah, I'm a real ray of sunshine today," popped out of her mouth before she knew it. "I'm sorry, Hunter."

"No harm, no foul." A look of concern crossed his face as he looked at her. "Is everything all right?"

"I didn't get much sleep last night, and let's just say it affected my baking so much that Lenora kicked me out." Why was she admitting this embarrassment to Hunter?

"Is your family well?" He stepped closer to the storefront to give more room to three men who were heading into the bakery.

Jillian wondered why he asked. She'd only known him a few months, but he wasn't the type to be scoping out whether she might soon need his services for Bertie or Cornelia. The twin sisters might be almost eighty years old, but they were both so full of life that she often forgot their age. Then she realized he was probably truly concerned about them. "Bertie and Cornelia are both fine. I'm sure they slept much better than I did."

"I'm glad to hear it. That they are well, not that you didn't sleep.

Can I walk you to your car?" he asked, ever the Southern gentleman.

Jillian had planned to keep her distance from Hunter after her grandmother and great-aunt had marked him as their choice for Jillian's first marriage from the day she had arrived back in Moss Hollow. But she had found the mortician to be too easygoing and funny to ignore. She tried to not be obvious about it when her family was nearby.

"Sure." She realized Hunter would be the perfect person to tell about Bridgett's journal. In his line of work, he knew how to keep a secret. "I'll even tell you why I lost sleep." As they strolled through the growing humidity of the morning, Jillian shared what she had found out since cleaning the attic with Savannah. Hunter listened closely, nodding and asking intelligent questions.

"Dupree, eh? That family has mostly passed on. Except Otis, of course."

Jillian nodded, a sheepish look on her face. "I was afraid of that. I remember Otis from twenty years ago. To be honest, I don't look forward to visiting him, but I have no other choice if I'm going to find out more about what happened after that night and beyond the years of Bridgett's journal."

A sympathetic chuckle came from Hunter. "We provided the funeral for Otis's last relative a few years ago. A cousin, Helen Blake. Otis caused quite a scene, ran off most everyone in record time. But I have a theory about that."

"Oh?" She put a Georgian inflection into her voice. "Do tell."

Hunter slowed as they approached her white Prius, the bright morning light revealing its need for a good wash, thanks to the country roads. "I noticed Otis was enjoying The Chocolate Shoppe's frosted cookies more than I've seen him enjoy anything, except maybe the peaches he grows. After he had eaten a few, other folks started helping themselves too. Wouldn't you know, that's when he started picking fights with everyone within hearing distance. Once he'd run most everyone off, he settled next to those cookies and had a feast."

"Did he now?" Jillian could have hugged Hunter for that piece of intel, but the Moss Hollow spy network was too much for her to face. She'd be hearing about it in thirty seconds flat, as would the entire town. "Thanks, Hunter. Now I can walk *you* back to the shop. I have some cookies to buy."

As she was boxing up a couple dozen frosted cookies, Lenora came through the kitchen door, pulling up short when she saw Jillian. "What are you up to now?"

"A good cause," Jillian answered meekly.

Lenora harrumphed. "It better be. Now get out of here before I put you to work again, far away from the bread."

Taking her longtime friend at her word, Jillian wasted no time making her selections and securing the box. On her way out, she waved to Hunter, who was sitting at a small table against the far wall. She hoped she'd have plenty to tell him the next time they met.

Jillian drove straight to the Dupree mansion before she could lose her nerve or her ability to drive from fatigue. She pulled through a heavy gate of a simple but striking design, the beauty of the old plantation home surprising her. It seemed incongruous for Otis to be such a curmudgeon while surrounded by such gracious architecture and lovely gardens. She always pictured him in a dark, crumbling house with ugly curtains.

Jillian parked her car in the wide stone circle at the front of the house, where a cascade of steps beckoned like open arms. The house was smaller than Belle Haven, but she had to admit it had been exquisitely maintained, something her family had been struggling to do for years, barely holding back the ravages of time.

She started toward the steps when a man stomped around the corner of the house. Wearing light-gray work clothes and heavy boots, he was bright red from his neck to his baldpate. Her foot froze on the first step. When he noticed her standing there like an awkward statue, he snapped, "Old man's crazy!" Before she could react, he flung open the door of his dark-green pickup and hightailed it out the gate, tires squealing.

She wondered if she should come back at a better time. Although, with Otis, Jillian suspected there was no such thing. But she had frosted cookies. If she left, she knew there was a good chance she'd eat them herself and not return. So she'd have to rely on the power of the sugary confections.

Jillian marched up the steps and rang the doorbell.

After some time, the door was opened by a housekeeper, her apron askew. "May I help you?"

Jillian had a sudden urge to offer the middle-aged woman the cookies. She looked like she might need them more. "I'm Jillian Green, from Belle Haven. I'd like to talk with Mr. Dupree, please."

The woman looked both relieved and a little worried.

Jillian showed her the box. "I've brought him some frosted cookies from The Chocolate Shoppe."

The corner of the housekeeper's mouth twitched, and she opened the door wider. "Come into the foyer while I announce you."

"Thank you." As soon as she stepped inside, Jillian found herself looking for the unsightly curtains she'd imagined would be in the house. There was not a single ugly one among the airy window coverings that seemed to welcome sunshine and breezes alike. The sight bolstered her confidence.

The quick footsteps of the housekeeper on the entry's marble floor announced her approach. "Mr. Dupree will see you in his study."

When Jillian entered the room, Otis was standing before a wide french window, staring outside and muttering.

"Here's Miss Green, Mr. Dupree," the housekeeper announced in a louder voice.

For a man with a cane, he pivoted swiftly. "Yes, I remember the girl's name, Dorothy." His pale-gray eyes settled on the box in Jillian's hand. "You can leave us."

Dorothy nodded without a word and slipped from the room.

The old man turned back to stare out the window. "Do you know anything about peach trees?"

"Not really," Jillian said. To her, the fruit trees she saw out the window seemed in perfect health, but that meant little.

"Neither does my groundskeeper, blast him." Otis thumped his cane onto the Persian rug under their feet. "He has no respect for the fine Georgia peach trees on my property. He's about as useless as a milk bucket under a bull."

"They certainly are fine trees." Jillian paused, already at the end of what she could contribute to the subject. Aunt Cornelia would know so much more. All she had were cookies and questions. "I brought you some frosted cookies from my grandmother's bakery." She opened the box, tilting it to show him the contents.

Otis's eyes narrowed for an instant, and Jillian braced herself for an outburst. But instead, he reached out a hand and scooped up several cookies with arthritically knobbed fingers. Dropping onto a long Chesterfield sofa, he gestured for her to sit beside him, no doubt to keep the cookies within grabbing distance.

Jillian tried not to focus on the shower of crumbs dropping down his shirt to settle into the tufting of the sofa. Dorothy must need a superpowered vacuum. "So you're Bertie's granddaughter, are you? How come I haven't seen you?"

"Yes, I am," Jillian answered. "I lived in another state for a couple of decades."

Otis jerked his head into a nod. "That's obvious from your accent. Are you going back soon?"

"No, I'm planning to stay in Moss Hollow." Jillian felt as if she were being grilled like salmon.

Otis grunted and reached for a second handful of cookies. After a couple minutes, he said, "I know a bribe when I see one. What do you want from me?"

She opened her mouth to protest but couldn't. "It's really more what I might be able to offer you, in the way of some information I discovered in the attic of Belle Haven."

She shared what she'd read about the friendly relations between the Belles and Duprees back in the 1860s.

"What does that have to do with me in the present?" Otis gave a gruff laugh. "I'm not a time traveler."

Jillian took a breath to steady herself before telling Otis what she'd read about that terrible night so long ago. "I've been wondering what happened to Jedediah and Bridgett, and to Frederick's family. Also, if Frederick's body is still buried at Belle Haven, please know I'd certainly be willing to help you arrange to have it moved wherever you prefer." Maybe if she offered to help the old man with Frederick's remains, he might be willing to help her learn about Jedediah and Bridgett, if he possessed that information.

Otis tightened his lips, trapping a lingering crumb in the process. "Again, this has nothing to do with me."

Jillian was aghast. "But Frederick was part of your family. Shouldn't his remains rest with your other departed family members, if he isn't yet?"

When Otis remained silent, she tried a slightly different tack. "Mr. Dupree, you have kept your home and grounds beautifully maintained. It's obvious you are knowledgeable about the history of your family home. If this information is new to you, I'd gladly share the old journal with you. And if you could share what you know about Frederick and Jedediah, I'd appreciate it greatly."

"Doesn't matter. There's nothing you can do for me, and I have nothing to tell you." He shoved himself up off the couch, limping over to a button next to a light switch and punching it with his thumb over and over. "You need to leave."

"But—"

"Dorothy!" Apparently, Otis wasn't sure the buzzer was working. "Dor-o-thy!" His Southern accent broadened as his volume went up.

The housekeeper ran into the study, breathless. "Yes, Mr. Dupree, what do you need?"

"I need you to move faster when I call. And I need a nap. Now." Otis was breathing even heavier than Dorothy.

With an apologetic glance her way, the housekeeper took Otis's arm. "Come along, then."

"If you ever want to see the journal, please let me know," Jillian said quickly before they could leave the room. "I'll leave my contact information on the desk."

Otis snorted. "Even if I wanted to find you, I wouldn't need your help. But I won't. And if you spread this around Moss Hollow, maybe Frederick Dupree won't be the only one buried at Belle Haven!"

With that, the old man again pivoted on his cane and stalked out of the room, the housekeeper trailing behind.

Jillian blew out a breath she hadn't realized she'd been holding. *Was that a threat?* She looked around the study. Maybe she could do a little snooping. Otis's study would be a logical place to start, with its desk, cabinets, and bookcases. But if the housekeeper caught her poking around, she'd have zero hope of Otis ever changing his mind. After another look at the peach orchard outside, wondering if Jedediah had tended any of it, she left the room.

She was crossing the marble floor toward the front door when she heard Otis yelling something about "that nosy girl." Well, nosiness was almost a mandated trait for Moss Hollow citizens. Perhaps she belonged here after all.

The adrenaline from her time with Otis Dupree drained from Jillian as she drove away, leaving her exhausted. Her early start gave her plenty of time for a nap, so she dragged herself up to her room as soon as she reached home. Once she could think straight again, she'd make a game plan to dig up as much information as she could on the Duprees. She kicked off her shoes, stretched out on her bed, and promptly fell asleep.

An hour later, Jillian woke up, her nose tickling. She opened her eyes and found herself looking into Possum's. "What are you doing here?" Had she been so tired when she'd come home that she hadn't closed her bedroom door all the way? Glancing at the clock, she decided that, this time, Possum's interference was helpful, keeping her from oversleeping. "Just don't make this a habit, got it?" Possum blinked at her and kneaded her shirt with his paws. Jillian caught the cat's paws in her hands. "Oh, no you don't. I don't need any pulls. I'm not your personal kitty mattress." Pulling back his captured paws, the cat jumped off Jillian and darted from the room.

Jillian got to her feet, stretching her arms over her head and leaning from side to side. She felt okay, surprisingly, and a glass of sweet tea would be just the thing to give her that little extra boost for her research.

Downstairs in the kitchen, she was filling a large glass with frosty tea when Bertie entered. Seeing Jillian, she crossed her arms and stared at her granddaughter. "Are you feeling better now?"

"A nap helped." Jillian lifted her glass. "Some sweet tea will finish the job."

"Lenora said you hadn't slept. What kept you up?" Bertie opened the refrigerator door and started pulling out food items. "You need some nourishment with that tea."

"No argument there." Jillian was still getting used to the differences between her former life as a single career woman in California and her new life with Bertie and Cornelia. But she couldn't complain about living with two great cooks who always kept a well-stocked kitchen. "As for what kept me up, I found something in the attic yesterday when Savannah and I were straightening up some stuff and dusting. Have you ever read the journal of Bridgett Summerlin?"

Bertie's hands were a blur as she chopped chicken, celery, walnuts, and red grapes for a quick chicken salad. "Why would I?"

"She lived here at Belle Haven for a while, visiting the Belles in 1861. I think she was their niece." Jillian set her glass on the counter and pulled two plates from the cupboard. "Her family lived in Tennessee, and she ended up staying for several months. I couldn't stop reading her journal last night, even though I had planned to get plenty of sleep. It was too interesting." She touched her grandmother's arm. "I'm sorry about the bread."

Bertie's eyes softened. "The customers were happy about the sandwich bread sale, but don't do it again. If you aren't up to doing something at the bakery, let us know. There are plenty of other things for you to do." She filled the plates with a mound of chicken salad on lettuce and crackers.

They carried their food to the breakfast area, where they ate all their meals. The huge dining room was too formal for the two sisters' tastes, and Jillian agreed. She dove into the chicken salad, realizing how long it had been since the biscuits and gravy. After a few mouthfuls, she paused. "Bertie, what kind of relationship is there between our family and the Duprees?"

Her grandmother looked up from her plate, her keen eyes guarded. "The Duprees? Why do you ask?"

"Bridgett writes about them, and it seemed like the two families were pretty close back then. I'm just curious." She didn't feel the need to describe how her bribery attempt had failed. "I've never seen Otis Dupree act remotely like his family had ever been on good terms with ours."

Bertie's face grew serious, and she pushed a small mound of chicken salad around her plate with a cracker. Jillian had never seen her grandmother play with her food. She used to constantly remind her granddaughter that "food items are not toys." Finally, she spoke. "All the joy in the Dupree family has slowly disappeared since Otis's mother died thirty years ago. Agnes was the glue holding the family together. One by one, Duprees have died, and now only Otis is left."

Jillian had hoped there might be another Dupree she could contact. Disappointed, she asked, "Do you know anything about the family in the late 1800s?"

Bertie shook her head. "The library has an old copy of *The History of Moss Hollow* and other regional books. You could try there or at the historical society, although you'll have to wait until Monday for that, since it is closed on weekends. And the library closes at five on Saturdays." She pointed a finger in Jillian's direction. "Don't stay up reading all night again. It's one thing to turn rustic dough into sandwich dough, but I won't have you sleeping during the sermon at church tomorrow."

"Don't worry, Bertie. My body won't let me. I'll be asleep early." Jillian glanced at the time. "If I leave now, I'll have a few hours to spend at the library." She stood, plate and glass in her hands. "Thanks for lunch and the suggestion." She leaned over, brushing a quick kiss on her grandmother's cheek.

When Jillian and her laptop walked through the door of the Moss Hollow Library, Annalise Reed greeted her. A member of the Southern Sweetie Pies baking club, along with Savannah, Lenora, Bertie, Cornelia, and other Moss Hollow women, Annalise also volunteered at the library. "I'm so excited about helping you with your baking at our meeting tomorrow, Jillian." She spoke over books stacked on a rolling cart.

Jillian wasn't sure if the Sweetie Pies could help her, but she resisted saying that to Annalise. Instead, she smiled. "If anyone can help, it's the Sweetie Pies." That was true. The number of lifetime baking hours most of the ladies in the group had was reassuring when she thought about it. "I need a different kind of help this afternoon. I need to do some research on the town's history."

"You came at the right time for that. The library's new reference librarian is here." Annalise's voice was quiet but animated, and her brown eyes sparkled. "Come and I'll introduce you." Leaving the cart, she took Jillian's arm and ushered her over to the smaller reference desk. A woman in her late forties was talking on the phone in a precise yet soft voice. "Yes, Dr. Linton, we do have that in our collection, and it's currently available for checkout . . . Certainly. You're welcome." She disconnected the call and lowered the handset. "Hi, Annalise."

"Jillian, this is Josi Rosenschein. She moved here with her brother, Albert, who's a semiretired general contractor. Josi, this is Jillian Green, Bertie Harper's granddaughter, who recently returned to Moss Hollow. She's been away for more than twenty years, so she's almost as new to most folks in town as you are." Annalise patted Jillian's hand as she spoke.

At least Annalise hadn't called her uppity like some people had when she'd first arrived. Josi stood to shake hands with Jillian, revealing she was about the same height as Jillian.

"Welcome to Moss Hollow, Josi. I hope you and your brother will be happy here." Jillian appreciated Josi's sense of style. Her taupe slacks and crisp white linen blouse were well cut and served as the perfect backdrop to the colorful necklace and bracelet she wore. Josi was the exact opposite of Annalise, who loved to don floral prints and stick with neutral accessories.

"Thank you, Jillian. We're enjoying the town very much. Annalise has been a great help, introducing me to all the local people and businesses."

"The Chocolate Shoppe being one of the first, of course," Annalise inserted. "But you weren't out front when we were there."

Josi nodded. "Oh, I'm sure I'll be a regular customer at your grandmother's shop. The orange cranberry scone I had was delicious. And you were selling some great sandwich bread today." Her hazel eyes were friendly with a hint of shyness, and Jillian found herself drawn to her, despite the inadvertent reference to her flopped dough. "Is there anything I can help you with today?"

"Actually, yes, there is." Before Jillian could continue, Annalise interrupted.

"I'll leave you in Josi's capable hands and get back to the book cart. It's not going to empty itself. See you tomorrow, Jillian." The plump woman bustled back to her work with an air of satisfaction.

Josi smiled and returned her focus to Jillian. "What exactly are you looking for?"

Jillian gave her a brief synopsis of her discovery and the information she hoped to find.

"I'm sure there are resources here that will help you." Josi's thin fingers tapped on her keyboard. "Most are available for checkout, and there's one in our rare book collection I can give you access to until closing." She stepped out from behind the desk, leading the way to the nonfiction stacks, a librarian on a mission in chunky green toe-capped heels.

Jillian followed behind Josi as she pulled several books from the shelves and handed them to her. Last, Josi took her to the Rare Book Room located behind the self-help section, unlocking it and switching on the light. Jillian had only been in the building a limited number of times since she had returned to Moss Hollow and didn't remember ever seeing that room before. She remembered more about the building when it housed Cooper's Pharmacy when she was a girl, when Bertie would buy her a milk shake from time to time.

The reference room was small but held a decent amount of resources for a small-town library. Josi moved to the shelves across from the door, efficiently scanning the top shelf and removing a large, clothbound book. "Here it is. *The History of Moss Hollow.* I'll set you up in a study room."

In minutes, Jillian was sitting in one of the tiny rooms reserved for private work that lined one side of the central library space with the books stacked around her. Flipping through each of them, she was relieved that she could check most of them out to take home. *The History of Moss Hollow* was her priority for this visit.

The heavy book, published initially in 1895, was subtitled *The First Hundred Years.* How could such a small place have so much history to record? Opening to the contents, her plan was to skip forward to the section labeled "War Between the States," but she stopped turning the pages when she saw the name Belle and then Belle Haven. Skimming as fast as she could, she was struck by the foundational role her ancestors played in the development of Moss Hollow through its history. The book described the building of Belle Haven by Captain Hoyt Belle in 1810, and the ball that was held there in 1824 to honor the Marquis de Lafayette for his assistance in the American Revolution during his final tour of the United States. Jillian was baffled. How did she not know this about her family's home? Her family had hosted a man who, six years later, would be offered, and would decline, the dictatorship of France during another of that country's revolutions!

Wow. Jillian made some notes in her laptop and moved ahead in time, pausing several times as a member of the Belle family was mentioned for his or her contribution to the community. There were also as many entries about the Duprees, often working together with the Belle family on civic improvement projects. With precious little time left before the library closed, she came to the "War Between the States" section to read that Vernon and Olive's son, Lewis, had quickly joined the fight and returned home as a decorated first lieutenant after spending several months in a Union prison. A few pages over, she found that Jedediah Dupree was discharged for wounds on August 2, 1861, and returned to Moss Hollow once he'd recuperated sufficiently for travel. While she felt relieved for his mother, not having to lose two sons in the span of a few short months, it also nagged at her that Jedediah had apparently not confessed to his crime against his brother. But how did he hide it from his parents? And what emotional conflict must Bridgett have battled, especially at such a tender age?

Jillian wondered if there had been any change in the relationship between the two families soon after the war. It seemed unlikely that Bridgett would have brought her aunt and uncle into her confidence about Frederick's demise and not have mentioned it in her journal, but Jillian flipped through more of the book, looking for clues. She found many references to both families and their work in the community, such as in 1893, when they both had been instrumental in the building of the first county hospital. The heads of the Belle and Dupree families had served on the first board of directors, and while Jillian supposed the two men could have served together while being estranged, it seemed unlikely that the writers of the history would have painted their collaboration in such glowing terms had they been at each others' throats.

It was looking more and more like Bridgett and Jedediah had both kept the events of that March evening between themselves. But if they had, it made no sense for Otis to have behaved the way he had. What was she missing? Had Otis reacted so fiercely simply out of his curmudgeon nature, or was there more to it than that?

Jillian was reading about a drive the Belles and Duprees had spearheaded to purchase the first motorized ambulance for the hospital when she heard Josi's voice over the intercom system. "Attention, patrons. The library will be closing in fifteen minutes. Thank you." She would have to return soon to continue searching for more of the book's secrets.

Gathering up all the books, she left the study room and took them all to the circulation desk, where Josi was checking out materials for the few remaining patrons.

When it was Jillian's turn, Josi scanned the regional history books for her, asking, "Did you find anything of interest yet? Sometimes research can be like mining for gold with a toothpick, but those exciting discoveries make it all worthwhile."

"I learned things I didn't know about my ancestors," Jillian admitted. "It never occurred to me that I'd find actual documentation about my family in a history book, even one that's just about Moss Hollow. Of course, I've barely scratched the surface, and the regional books might not contain anything useful. But that won't keep me from looking."

Josi placed the last book on top of the pile. "That's a wise plan. When scholars are researching for books, they delve into all the minutiae they can find. Store receipts, minutes of town hall meetings, diaries, local newspapers, letters—almost anything that has survived can reveal something. And each researcher has his or her own personality that mingles with the methods. Something that seems irrelevant to many historians may spark a connection in one and become the focal point of an article, a chapter, or a book. One of them could have found some of your family's papers from stores or trades people, or a tutor even, along the way and included it in a book. I hope you find what you're looking for."

Jillian handed over *The History of Moss Hollow.* "Thanks. I'll be back to study this one more someday soon. There are some fascinating stories in it."

"Excellent." Josi set the book to the side. "See you tomorrow at the Sweetie Pies meeting."

Oh goodie, another witness to my culinary ineptitude. Jillian suddenly felt relieved knowing that the Sweetie Pies didn't keep minutes of their meetings for some future historian to cull through. "I'm sure you'll enjoy it. It's hard not to when the meetings revolve around eating delicious treats and exchanging recipes." She waved good-bye to Annalise as she turned toward the front doors. "Have a good night."

Even with her arms full of books, she was still drawn to stop at the window of The Dusty Magnolia antique shop a few doors down from the library. Inside, she saw a pair of cabinets that looked similar to one she had noticed in the Belle Haven attic with wavy glass set in the sliding doors. But unlike that one, these were absolutely gorgeous, the finish restored beautifully. The cabinet sported hooks rather than shelves, and Jillian had wondered what it was made for. Shifting the books onto a hip, she leaned close to the storefront glass and peered at the description card tucked into one of the glass panes.

It read, "Set of two French tack cabinets. Original finish and glass. $35,000 for the set." *What? Almost $18,000 for just one of those cabinets?* Surely with some elbow grease to restore the finish and polish the hardware, maybe exchange the hooks for shelves, she could use the similar-looking cabinet that was tucked away in the attic of Belle Haven to perk up one of the mansion's rooms that had become rather dingy over the decades. She and Savannah had seen so many intriguing pieces during their attic foray; they could significantly improve the interior of Belle Haven with a little ingenuity and work.

In the middle of her planning, an angry voice shouted, almost in her ear. "That old cur!" Although her heart skipped, Jillian stayed motionless, staring at the reflection of the man in the storefront glass just a few feet down the sidewalk. A thin man in a blue business suit bared his teeth as he stared at the phone in his hand. He reminded Jillian of a ferret. "He won't mess with me again when I'm done," Ferret-Man vowed. He jammed the phone into his suit pocket and growled as he began moving again. Jillian turned and watched as the man disappeared around the corner, still ranting.

"Dupree will pay for this!"

Jillian awoke the next morning to sunshine and a refreshing breeze that danced through her open window. As a child, she had always felt mornings like this were her reward for suffering through the long, hot summers.

After returning home from the library the evening before, Jillian had been tempted to fall right into bed, but she'd wanted to focus on the threat that the ferret-faced man had made toward Otis Dupree. She knew that Otis could be a pain in the bread dough, but what could he have done to this person to evoke such bald hatred? Should she call the sheriff's office and report the outburst? But what good would that do? Otis probably had his share of enemies.

After devoting some time to those thoughts, she'd forced herself to eat some dinner, then held off her bath until nine o'clock. The result was one of the best nights of sleep she'd had in years.

Resting her elbows on the windowsill, she gazed out over the flower beds Cornelia tended to so diligently. She'd never tell her great-aunt, but sometimes it was hard to believe Cornelia didn't possess some kind of garden-keeping magic. If she ever said anything like that to Bertie, her grandmother would likely scoff and respond with one of her wise retorts. "Don't mix up magic for plenty of good old-fashioned work and a gift from God." Bertie was right, of course, and Jillian intended to start her day outside enjoying it.

She slipped into a soft pair of jeans and a long-sleeved shirt of lightweight material. The day would heat up soon enough, and then she would change into short sleeves. But long sleeves were perfect now for an early morning walk. Before leaving her room, she reread Bridgett's journal about Frederick's burial to remind her of any detail that might help her find the location. It amounted to a "large live oak" and "back acreage." Those clues were thinner than a stingy man's grits, but she'd have to make do.

On the way out, she popped into the kitchen to make some toast from the extra loaf of sandwich bread in the bread box. Good thing she had prepared all of that sandwich bread dough. She carried it with her, nibbling as she wandered through the pathways to the back of the main house. Bridgett had written about how Frederick had died when he'd struck his head against a fountain. Was that the same fountain a confused man had defaced when he'd tried to shoot her last summer? If it was, for such a lovely fountain, it bore a grisly history. At least it was a place to start.

As she waded through the wild overgrowth toward the presently dry water feature, she wondered how far Jedediah and Bridgett had been able to carry Frederick's body. They were both young, and Jedediah had not yet been wounded, but Belle Haven before and during the Civil War had been a vast plantation of hundreds of acres. The ten acres of her family's property that remained was but a postage stamp compared to what it had been. Bridgett had written "back acreage." What if the body no longer rested on Belle Haven land?

Jillian slowly paced around the fountain, picturing that night so long ago. *Did he fall here? Or there?* Was that spot on the stone rim rust or very old blood? *The History of Moss Hollow* had mentioned the splendor of Belle Haven in its chapter about Lafayette's visit and had used the words "gracious fountains." Plural. Where were those other fountains? Were they now on other people's properties?

And the trees. Jillian cast her gaze over the acreage, as far as she could see. There was a whole stand of live oak trees, so that clue wasn't helpful. She could dig under each one every day and be mighty old before finding Frederick's grave. But that was only if it was still on their land.

Maybe Savannah knows something about the people who bought some of the parcels of the original Belle Haven plantation. She pulled out her cell phone and called her friend, but it went to voice mail. After leaving a message, she spotted the largest tree she'd seen yet, and that was saying something. Striding toward it, she was reminded of a book she'd read as a child, about a boy who had run away from home and took up residence in the hollow of a giant tree. This tree would have made that boy a spacious tree house.

She stared at the bark, looking for any unusual markings, in case Jedediah had wanted to find it later. She stared at the roots, wondering if they'd grown around Frederick like a free-form coffin.

"Jiiillliiiaaan!" a voice called, making her jump. She turned to see Cornelia picking her way through the path of trodden grass Jillian had made. "My, you had a wandering spirit this morning, didn't you?"

Her great-aunt often used an uncanny choice of words. Jillian felt the hint of a chill creep along her spine. "I just wanted to enjoy the cool morning. It's been a long time since we've had one." Cornelia stood in front of the massive oak, becoming still and silent for a full minute. "Aunt Cornelia, are you okay?"

The older woman reached out a hand and laid it on the bark of the tree, her gnarled gardener hands almost camouflaged by the rough bark. "Huh?" She gave a little shake of her head. "I'm fine, dear. There's just something about this tree I hadn't noticed before. But there's no time." She turned back to Jillian. "We're leaving for church in twenty-five minutes. You'll want to get ready."

So that's why Savannah hadn't answered. She was probably getting ready for church too. Jillian hoped they'd be able to talk after the service. She linked arms with Cornelia. "Thanks for letting me know. I lost track of time." And the day, for that matter. "At least I had a nice bath last night; changing will be fast."

"Yes, I know. I drew myself a bath later in the evening, plunging in to find the water colder than the old springhouse water."

"Oh, Cornelia, I'm so sorry. I didn't realize." The water had been pleasantly warm for her bath, which should have been her clue that she'd tapped out the ancient water heater.

Her great-aunt patted her arm. "Don't give it another thought. I've read that a good dousing of frigid water is excellent for the circulatory system. The people in those freezing European countries do it all the time. Why should they have all the fun?"

Cornelia had been surprising Jillian regularly since she'd returned to Belle Haven. Her *joie de vivre* was often contagious. "You're something else."

Her great-aunt looked puzzled. "But I haven't changed for quite some time, Jillian. Now, my sweet Raymond, he has changed. In the twinkling of an eye." She turned around to look at the massive oak. Glancing over her shoulder, Jillian saw Possum digging around a rope of exposed root. "And I think he's going to send us a message soon."

"I think he's going to send you a field mouse soon," Jillian said. "Bertie will love that."

As soon as they reached the house, Jillian ran up the stairs to brush out her hair and pull on a bell-sleeved shift dress in a dark-green geometric print. While the humidity was still much higher than she had been used to in California, it had moderated enough to almost return the frizz factor of her hair to neutral, with a little help from a Southern-certified hair product from Lenora's cousin, Jasmine Jackson at the Clip & Curl hair salon.

She was back downstairs in time to save Bertie the oxygen of shouting up to her to get a move on and not keep the pastor waiting. *As though he would hold off the sermon just for me.* They walked through the wide double doors of Moss Hollow Fellowship Church with time to spare for fellowship—or to dissect the fashion choices of those around them, as some in the congregation were wont to do. Jillian glanced around the pews, searching the faces for Savannah. As usual, she found her friend near the front, sitting beside their childhood buddy and Jillian's first boyfriend from high school, James Wilson.

"Hi, James." He'd been through some rough times, and some folks of Moss Hollow were having a hard time putting it behind them. But to Jillian, he was still her friend and always would be, like Savannah.

James looked more relaxed than she'd seen him since she'd returned to town. "Hey, Jillian. What's up?"

She raised a hand in greeting. "Nothing much. How're things with you?"

"Good. Can't complain," he replied with a smile.

She turned to her best friend. "Savannah, I called you a while ago so just ignore my message, but let's talk after the service, okay?"

"Even better, why don't you come over for lunch after church?" her friend said. "You can come home with me, and we can go to the Sweetie Pies meeting together."

Across the aisle, Bertie was giving her the stink eye, and Jillian realized Pastor Keith was walking toward the front of the church. "Sounds good. Gotta go." She slipped across to the pew where Bertie and Cornelia always sat, sinking down next to Cornelia. Immediately, she bowed her head, taking a few breaths to refocus her mind on the reason they were there. Avoiding any of Bertie's expressive looks was simply a pleasant side benefit.

Pastor Keith preached on John 14:27. The church bulletin listed the title of the sermon: "Peace, Peace, God's Peace." She joyfully sang the chorus of the final hymn, "It Is Well with My

Soul," and after Pastor Keith had dismissed the congregation, she let Bertie and Cornelia know she was going to Savannah's. Bertie had gotten over her stink eye, and she only reminded Jillian not to be late for the Sweetie Pies meeting. Funny how her grandmother's admonishments either pricked her like porcupine quills or reminded her that she was cared for, depending on her state of mind. This time, she smiled. "Savannah doesn't like to be late for anything, so we'll be right on time, if not early." She noticed Josi standing partway down the aisle and went to greet her.

Beside the new librarian stood a middle-aged man with light hair that was turning to gray. It reminded Jillian of a hayfield after a light snow. "Hello, Josi. I didn't realize you attended church here. Welcome."

The librarian's face lit up at her greeting. "This is our first time. We've slowly been sampling all the churches in the area. I really liked the music selections and sermon." She turned to the man beside her. "This is my brother, Albert. Jillian's family owns Belle Haven, that gorgeous plantation house we saw the other day."

Albert's brown eyes brightened, and he reached out his right hand. "I'm pleased to meet you, Miss . . ."

"Green, but please call me Jillian, or I'll feel like an old-maid schoolteacher," she said, surprised at how deep Albert's voice was. "Are you interested in antebellum architecture?"

"Yes, I am. I worked on several plantation mansions during my years as a general contractor. These days, I'm focusing on restoration of historic buildings and homes, now that I'm working for myself and deciding which projects I want to pursue."

Here was a man with a passion for his work. It highlighted to Jillian how long she had remained in her marketing career after the initial excitement had cooled. It had been a long time since her eyes had sparkled like Albert's. More and more, the humiliation of her career's demise was looking less like a tragedy and more like an opportunity for positive change.

"You should have your pick of interesting projects in this part of the state, then," she said. "We have more historical buildings than you can shake a stick at." She noticed Savannah lingering by the door. "I need to be on my way, but it's been nice meeting you. And I hope you'll come back next week. Josi, I'll see you later at the Sweetie Pies meeting."

She hurried toward the back of the sanctuary. "Sorry, I wanted to speak to Josi so she would feel welcome. Her brother seemed nice too."

"No problem. I just finished talking with folks myself."

After thanking Pastor Keith for the encouraging sermon, the two women left the church, arriving at Savannah's home a few minutes later. The bungalow was tiny compared to Belle Haven, but the cheerful, light-yellow paint and white trim seemed to welcome visitors like a friendly smile. Inside, the honey-colored wooden floors had been meticulously refinished, and Savannah had chosen furniture that was both comfortable and pleasing to the eye without a single froufrou item cluttering up the space.

Jillian dropped her purse onto the small arts and crafts table near the front door. "Did you refinish your floors? I mean, actually do the job?"

"Yes, I did, and 'job' is the right word to use. It was a huge project. I watched every online video I could, read home-remodeling magazines, pestered the experts at Puckett's Hardware store, and consulted Mrs. Toombs at The Dusty Magnolia about a hundred times to make sure I wasn't ruining the patina of the original floors." Her eyes lovingly skimmed across the results. "It was worth every pain. I love how it turned out."

"As you should," said Jillian, "because they're beautiful. And it's funny you mentioned The Dusty Magnolia." She told her about the French tack cabinets she'd seen and her new plan for restoring some of the furniture. "My condo in California was modern, so I'm out of my league in the refinishing department. Would you be willing to help me? It's one way I can help Bertie and Cornelia."

Savannah led the way into the kitchen, which was a little wider than galley style but with a design that utilized every inch of the small space, so it felt much larger. "Sure. Furniture is much easier on the knees." She opened the refrigerator and took out a large bowl of salad.

"That looks delicious," Jillian crooned. "So where is your bowl?"

"Ha-ha." Savannah reached back into refrigerator for a carafe of dressing. "I hope you like red pepper and garlic."

"I don't think I've ever had that." Jillian eyed the bottle. "It looks almost like a French dressing."

"It has a sweet and savory balance with a little kick." Saying, "And just so you don't forget, you're in the South," Savannah took a cloth cover off a plate of corn bread. Handing Jillian a crock of butter and a honey pot, she carried the corn bread and salad to the small dining room between the kitchen and living room.

Once they were settled down to eat, Jillian continued where their conversation had left off. "I'm so relieved you are willing to help with the furniture; I can't wait to surprise Bertie and Cornelia with the finished pieces." She skimmed the thinnest layer of butter on a square of corn bread. "Oh, I saw something else surprising at The Dusty Magnolia. Some*one*, actually."

As soon as she described the ferret-faced man she'd seen in the glass and what he had said, Savannah gasped and covered her mouth.

"What?" Jillian asked, noticing her friend's face was turning red. "Are you all right? Make the universal choking sign if you need the Heimlich maneuver." She was really getting worried, ready to spring into action, when Savannah dropped her hand and gasped enough air to laugh out loud. "Have mercy, Savannah! I thought you were choking to death."

"I'm sorry." Her friend's voice came out in spurts between giggles. "Maybe it shouldn't be so funny. I always thought Ted Grady looked like an animal but could never quite put my finger on which one." Her breathing calmed a little, and she took a deep breath. "You nailed it. He does look like a ferret."

"Ted Grady?" Jillian asked. "What's his story? Do you have any idea why he'd be threatening to make Otis pay?"

"I don't know what Ted was yelling about specifically, but there's a long history between him and Otis, for sure." Savannah paused to sip her tea before continuing. "Ted is a town councilman. He first ran for office eight years ago but didn't win. Then, before the next election, he convinced Otis to fund and back his campaign. I don't know what exactly Ted promised in exchange, but I know Otis believed he was buying himself a Dupree politician."

Jillian shook her head as she dipped a forkful of salad into the richly colored dressing. "After my visit with Otis and being reminded of his dubious charms, I have trouble seeing how his support could win an election for anyone. Especially not for someone who resembles a polecat crossed with a weasel."

"Well, from what I've heard, Otis started out fairly well-liked when he was younger. He just got meaner as he aged."

"Bertie said he really went downhill after his mother died." Jillian found it difficult to relate, as her own mother had been too flighty to contribute much to her upbringing.

Savannah drizzled some honey over her corn bread. "Exactly. So some of the older people who still remembered what Otis was like when he was young listened to him out of pity. But the vast majority listened out of fear because Otis became very good at digging up dirt on people and using it to control them."

"Ugh, I got off light, then," said Jillian. "He merely left me to take his nap without so much as a grain of information about Jedediah or Frederick. You'd think he'd be interested in knowing that one of his ancestors might be buried at Belle Haven." Her eyes narrowed. "Do you think Otis found some dirt on Ted and used it against him?"

Savannah fingered her glass. "Oh, I'm sure Otis has a fat old file on our councilman. You see, after Ted was elected, he didn't act like Otis's puppet, as I'm sure was expected of him."

"He went rogue on Otis?" Jillian leaned forward, whistling.

"We've all had a front-row seat to their feud ever since. I'd appreciate Ted's rebellion against that ornery old goat, but the truth is, he's just as unethical as the old man."

Jillian settled her fork on the rim of her plate. "I'd sure like to know what Otis did to Ted this time."

"You and every other busybody in town," Savannah teased. "Myself included."

"Maybe Otis is in a better mood now since he's apparently struck a blow to Ted." Jillian's fingers tapped lightly on the cheerful tablecloth. "I think I'll pay him another visit tomorrow. Maybe this time he'll be willing to talk."

Savannah lifted her shoulders. "You never know with Otis. But you can be sure that if he gives you any help, he'll expect to get something in return, one way or another. So be careful."

A little shiver flickered down her spine. "I will." Jillian checked the time. "Did you make anything for the meeting yet? Bertie told me to remind you it was your turn to bring the treat."

"Yes, I made a chocolate espresso Bundt cake."

"Where were you and that cake when I needed it so much? Did you print the recipe cards yet?"

"I made them while you were trying to sweet-talk Otis. Want to see?" Savannah got up from the table, disappearing into the living room. She returned with a small, neat card and handed it to Jillian.

The card was perfectly formatted and perfectly written. It was also perfectly boring. "Oh." She tried to sound enthusiastic. "Oh, look. It has espresso in it."

"What's wrong?" Savannah bent over to peer at the card. "I didn't miss a typo, did I?"

"Nope, every word is correct, and the recipe is clear and concise. It just doesn't match your personality or the feel of the recipe. Do you know what I mean?"

Savannah cocked her head to the side. "I never thought of the recipe cards that way before, but I see what you mean."

"Did you save the template on your computer?" Jillian asked. When her friend nodded, she said, "If you'd like, I could help you spruce it up a little. Make it more 'Savannah,' just like you did with your house."

Savannah started clearing the table. "Let's clean up fast and get to it! This might be fun."

Later, when Jillian and Savannah entered The Chocolate Shoppe, Bertie and Cornelia were chatting with Annalise and Josi. Savannah carried the Bundt cake in on a blue-splatter stoneware plate with a glass dome cover to display her contribution and set it on the counter. "Are Laura Lee and Lenora coming?" she asked.

"As far as we know," Annalise answered. "It's still a few minutes early." She floated away from the others to examine the treat for the afternoon. "This looks lovely, Savannah. I hope you didn't forget the recipe cards, if it tastes as good as it looks."

Cornelia gave a trilling laugh. "Savannah forget her cards? She's far too organized." She waved Savannah over. "Josi, have you met Savannah yet?"

Josi smiled shyly and nodded. "I have. Annalise introduced us after I mentioned my brother would need a new bookkeeper for his business. We're so relieved Savannah could take on another client."

"Our Savannah is a woman of many talents," Cornelia said, handing everyone a plate.

Jillian wondered what Josi thought of Cornelia's use of the possessive "our." There were two sides of that coin in her recent experience: support and pressure.

Her great-aunt continued, "All she's lacking is a husband, but I'm sure that will be resolved before too long." She was smiling until she glanced over at Bertie. "Sister, are you having a stroke? Your eyes have gone all catawampus."

"Newcomers shouldn't be burdened with certain information," Bertie snapped. "What's past is past."

"Since when?" Jillian blurted. "You certainly felt free to burden me with plenty of information as soon as I arrived." Mostly pertaining to the history and eligibility of a certain handsome mortician, but she wasn't going to redirect her grandmother's attention onto that overplayed tune.

Bertie rolled her eyes, like she did whenever her sister mentioned anything about haints. "You're different, of course. You're a *native.*" She marched over to the counter and picked up the serving knife, flourishing it in Josi's direction.

Cornelia gasped. "Bertie, you're going too far."

Her sister lifted the glass dome from the cake and started vigorously slicing generous portions. "What are you going on about, Cornelia? I only meant that Josi has enough to deal with in setting up her new home, taking care of her brother, and learning the new routine of a different library. She'll have plenty of time to get to know folks and for folks to get to know her." She took a piece of cake that barely fit on its plate over to the librarian. "And Savannah is a fine person to know."

Josi looked a bit dazed but managed to speak. "I'm looking forward to getting to know as many people as I can." She took a petite bite of the cake and turned to Savannah. "This cake is amazing. I'm definitely going to make this for Al."

Jillian jumped at the chance to redirect the conversation, even though it could be like herding cats with this group. "I enjoyed meeting your brother this morning. He seems so dedicated to his work."

Annalise's fork paused a few inches from her mouth. "Oh, he really is. I asked him to repair some old newel posts in our house. They can be tricky, you know, with the house being so old, though not as old as Belle Haven. And we couldn't be more pleased with the results. My husband, Byron, even suggested asking Albert to tackle some other projects around our place that he's been putting off for so many years. I was considering cross-stitching a honey-do list onto his pillow."

The shop door suddenly opened, and Laura Lee Zane strode through. Laura Lee was a deputy in the sheriff's office, so the Sweetie Pies were used to her coming in after the start of a meeting. It went with the job.

"I'm so sorry I'm late. I was heading out the door when I had to go out on a call."

"Oh. What happened?" Cornelia asked.

Laura Lee made a beeline for the cake and helped herself. "It was just a minor fender bender out on Old Quarry Road." With an apologetic look at Bertie, she continued her story. "Larry Roberts made a wide right turn with his cattle trailer and clipped Roy Jackson's new truck." She shook her head. "At least no one was hurt, and they didn't come to blows over the incident."

Bertie nodded. "Well, forget about that now. As Southern women we must strive to let go of the unessential bits in life and focus on what's needful." She primly took a small bite of cake, as though imitating the newest member of the group.

Jillian wondered what her grandmother's definition of "needful" was and felt certain it differed from her own.

"I think it's needful for Savannah to give us her recipe card," said Laura Lee.

Wiping her already-clean hands on a napkin, Savannah retrieved the revised cards from her purse and handed them around.

"Thank you, Savannah," Cornelia said, taking a card. She started to tuck it right into her skirt pocket but did a double take after catching a glimpse of it. "Why, you've changed your card design. It's wonderful."

All the women gathered around Savannah, exclaiming over the miniature bungalow with a pie sitting on a windowsill.

"I can't take the credit for this," she confessed. "Jillian put her mad designing skills to work, improving my boring template."

Jillian countered, "I never said it was boring." She'd thought it, but she hadn't said it. "Yours was perfectly . . . adequate."

Savannah didn't reply but turned her head enough away from Bertie's line of vision to give Jillian the smallest of winks.

"You know, Bertie," Annalise said, "if you hired Albert to restore some of the rooms of Belle Haven, and if Jillian used her marketing experience, I think you might be able to hold events out there. Weddings, reunions, and the like. We really don't have a place for things like that in Moss Hollow. It could supplement the income from The Chocolate Shoppe quite handsomely."

In her almost eighty years of life, Bertie had always preferred to be the one to initiate action, to take charge. But she simply responded, "I'll think about it."

Jillian turned to Josi. "Why don't you give me Albert's business number?"

Bertie's sharp eyes watched her, but she ignored it.

"Sure." Josi pulled a card from her colorful paisley purse and held it out. "Please don't feel obligated, but Al really does treat all historical homes like precious treasures. Oh." She took the card back and pulled out a pen. "I'll jot down where you can see some photos of Albert's work on the Internet." She paused, printing quickly, and held it out to Jillian again.

Jillian turned over the card, thinking of Otis. This was her excuse to return to the Dupree mansion. Although Otis took no notice of the people he used as pawns for his own plans, clearly the plantation was dear to him. If bribing him with his favorite cookies didn't work, perhaps introducing him to Albert's expertise would.

Jillian sat on the veranda, enjoying her coffee and watching Possum stalk from flower bed to flower bed, pouncing on anything that moved, including a red hibiscus petal that dropped off the bush.

Thankfully, Cornelia had already left or she would have insisted her late husband was warning her of some grave danger through Possum by shredding the red blossom with his claws. Instead, Cornelia was off to Miss Jasmine's beauty salon, the Clip & Curl. Before she left, Cornelia had explained to Jillian that as soon as the Georgia temperatures dropped below ninety degrees, the women of Moss Hollow started thinking about the coming holidays, which led to thinking about trying new hairstyles, which led to a crowded salon.

"So you go early to beat the crowd?" Jillian had asked.

"Of course not." Cornelia had laughed as she adjusted her hat. "What fun is an empty salon? Everyone goes early to be ready for all the fall events, of course. The picnics, hayrides, festivals, errands around town, and such. Before they're too tired for gossip."

Having been back in Georgia for some time now, Jillian was pretty sure Moss Hollow citizens always had energy for gossip, no matter the temperature or humidity, but she'd kept her opinion to herself and Cornelia had departed.

The door opened, and Bertie stepped onto the veranda, not stopping until she reached the edge. She stood there silently with her arms folded over her chest and stared. Not at the lovely landscaping her sister had created, but down at the woodwork and column pedestal. "Is everything all right, Bertie?" Jillian asked.

Her grandmother sighed and then shook herself. "Annalise called to repeat her suggestion that we hire Albert Rosenschein to help restore Belle Haven." She closed her eyes briefly and opened them again. "I've worked hard to keep our family home as maintained as possible under our circumstances."

"And you and Cornelia have shown your priorities by giving all you have to keeping the house functioning," said Jillian. "It's a huge task."

"I know I don't have the expertise to do everything that needs to be done. But if I hire someone—no matter how glowing his or her credentials might be—who might unintentionally harm any part of Belle Haven, I'd never forgive myself."

"What is it you used to tell me when I was younger?" Jillian smiled. "'Worryin' gives small things big shadows.' Let's not worry about something that hasn't even happened." Her grandmother had always had the tendency to carry too much on her shoulders, and no matter her strength of spirit, it could weigh her down. "You also used to say, 'Never trouble trouble 'til trouble troubles you.'"

"Hmm." Bertie tried to look stern, but there was a twinkle in her eye. "Good to know you were listening."

Jillian thought for a moment. "Since Annalise recommends Albert so highly after his work on her home, what if we ask Albert to come to Belle Haven while all three of us are here and talk about a few straightforward projects? We can ask him as many questions as we want, and if we all agree, hire him for those few projects. Then we can watch how he treats the house and his work, and decide if we would like him to do more."

The soft lines between Bertie's eyes deepened as she thought. "You have a sensible plan there. Call and ask Albert if he can come on Wednesday, preferably midmorning since you'll be at the shop for the early rush."

"I'll call as soon as I finish breakfast," Jillian promised. "I did a bit of searching on the Internet last night to see if I could find any negative reviews about his work or how he conducts business."

"And?"

She gave a small shrug. "I didn't find any. There wasn't time for an exhaustive search, but on the surface, he seems very legit."

"I'm glad you checked."

"You know, the idea Annalise had about us catering events here at Belle Haven could really work for us."

"How so?"

"Well, weddings require cakes, and reunions need goodies of all sorts. We could make Belle Haven into something people would want to use. The profits from the rentals would augment our proceeds from the bakery. We might even be able to remodel some of the unused rooms and take in overnight guests, bed-and-breakfast style."

Bertie's arms dropped to her sides, and she traced the outline of the pedestal beside her. "It's something to think about, I suppose. Thank you, Jillian. I'll keep it in mind, but for now I've got to get to the bakery."

"I'll be there for the lunch and after-school rush," Jillian said. "I have some errands to run this morning."

After her grandmother drove off, Jillian finished her eggs and grits, and then called Albert. When the call went to voice mail, she left a brief message with her cell number, reminding him of their brief conversation on Sunday. Shortly after that, she drove to the Dupree mansion.

She stood before the massive double doors for a long time, knocking repeatedly and ringing the bell. Living in a sprawling home herself, she understood it could take Dorothy some time to move from farther wings of the house to the main door, but after so many minutes had passed, she became curious. Maybe the housekeeper had gone out on an errand.

Jillian waited a couple of minutes before weighing her options. If she walked around to the back, maybe she would find Otis in his study and could gain entrance through the room's French windows.

Since she had seen peach trees from the study's windows, she went looking for them in order to find the correct wing of the sprawling building. Bridgett's journal had mentioned the Dupree peach orchard. After watching Otis's zeal for the fruit trees on Saturday, she found herself paying close attention to them. She also wondered if she'd find the groundskeeper back at work after his angry display the other day. On their way to the Southern Sweetie Pies meeting, Savannah had put a name to the red face—Harold Johnson—and encouraged her not to make hasty conclusions about him after one experience, so Jillian supposed she'd listen to her friend. If Harold happened to be working in the orchard, perhaps he would tell her if Otis was at home.

Following along the back of the house bordering the fruit trees, she found the study. She approached the windows slowly so as not to startle the older man. When she didn't see any movement inside, she dared to lean closer to the glass, shading both sides of her face from the glare of the morning sunshine. Realizing the room was empty, she turned away, disappointed. After peeking into several other windows and doors, she decided to go looking for Harold farther into the orchard.

She was picturing Jedediah behind every tree and Bridgett walking with Mrs. Dupree on her first visit to the plantation. As she approached the outer bounds of the trees, she saw a ladder leaning against one of the trees. Perhaps she'd finally found Harold. She walked softly but picked up her pace when she saw something stretched out on the ground. Then she ran.

Otis! One leg tucked under him and his arms outstretched, he lay as still as a statue. She didn't have to listen to his chest to know he was dead.

Jillian dropped to her knees beside Otis, staring at his pale, still face that she'd last seen full of energy. Intensely negative energy, but that was more natural than what she saw now.

Digging into her pocket for her phone, she dialed 911 with shaking fingers and informed the dispatcher of her discovery. After giving the necessary information, she backed away from Otis's body and looked around her, feeling the need to pace. The cane Otis had had with him during her visit was close, propped against the tree with the ladder. She pictured the old man as he had gripped it, flourishing it angrily at times. She leaned close to get a better look. Underneath the brass lion head, she noticed a tiny button. She didn't want to leave any prints on it in case Otis's death had not been accidental, but she suddenly, and desperately, wanted to know what the button did. Wrapping the fingers of one hand in her blouse, Jillian braced the cane against the tree with her leg and pressed the button.

There was a *shhhnick* sound and a thin but deadly looking blade pushed into the dirt from the bottom of the cane, making Jillian jump back. Once her breathing had slowed again, she pushed the button again and watched in grim fascination as the weapon retracted. Seeing the weapon made her mind race, and she searched along the ground for any sign of blood. Otis looked to be free from obvious wounds, but she wasn't going to lift his head to make sure. If an intruder with more ominous intent than hers had approached him, perhaps Otis had used his cane.

Except that his cane was propped against the tree and not within his grasp where he was sprawled.

Jillian rubbed her face. She needed to calm down. *Here's a thought: I can let the sheriff's department handle it.* Leaving the cane against the tree, she began to pace and found herself following Harold Johnson's footprints, as though tracking his workdays among the fruit trees. After a few minutes, she realized she was looking at two different sets of prints. She squatted down to examine them more closely. The two sets seemed to be the same size, but there was something different about the second pair. Jillian couldn't put her finger on it, though, so she took some photos with her phone. Whoever answered the emergency call would probably be able to see the difference, since in their line of work, details were important.

Don't get ahead of yourself, Jillian, she warned herself. *You're just spooked by Otis's cane, that's all.* She focused on taking long, deep breaths until she heard the sirens of the emergency vehicles. When she heard the voice of Deputy Sheriff Goodman Jones—Gooder to the people of Moss Hollow—through the trees, she waved her arms and shouted, "Over here!"

She watched the tall deputy direct the ambulance as it bounced through the rows of trees until it stopped a few yards away from Otis's body.

"Are you making this a habit, Jillian?"

Her mouth dropped open. "I assure you this is the first time I've discovered a dead person." Why couldn't Laura Lee Zane have been the deputy to arrive, instead of someone she'd known in high school and who had annoyed her on other unfortunate occasions?

The deputy's green eyes stared into hers as the emergency medical technicians knelt beside the body. "What were you doing here, and how did you come to find the body?"

"I had a history question I wanted to ask Otis." She kept her statement as vague as possible. "When I knocked on the front door several times and the housekeeper didn't answer, I thought I'd look for Harold or Otis in the orchard. I noticed the ladder first and came to see if either of them was here. That's when I found the body."

Gooder narrowed his eyes. "I didn't realize you were on such friendly terms with Otis Dupree to come calling with any question, much less one about history. I don't remember you being interested much in history."

"And I don't remember you being fit with broad shoulders either," she snapped. "But you changed. Why can't I? Besides, what's so strange about it? Both of our families were early settlers of Moss Hollow." Jillian hoped her last statement might distract the deputy from her initial response. She should have stuffed that one in her mouth before it got out. But the stress of finding a dead body was really getting to her.

The officer's nostrils flared. "Because the Belles and the Duprees haven't socialized for a long time."

"What do you know about that?" she asked, turning the grill back on Gooder. Seriously, what did he know? So far she hadn't found any information about that from the library books.

He shrugged stiffly. "I can't recall witnessing any interaction between either your grandmother or great-aunt and Otis in the fifteen years I've been in the department. Or before that either."

"Well, since I wasn't here during those years, I wouldn't know that." Jillian debated how much to say, since she didn't know if it would add confusion to the investigation, if there even needed to be an investigation. "I only wanted to share something with him that I found in the attic of Belle Haven that pertained to his ancestors, that's all." She didn't feel the need to mention the body reportedly buried under the live oak. Then she remembered the footprints. "But I found something you need to look at." She grabbed his arm.

He shook her off gently. "Of course you did." He swept the surrounding area with his eyes. "Where?"

She led him over to the two sets of footprints. "See?"

Gooder stared at the ground and raised his eyebrows. "So? Prints from workman boots. Do you know how many hours every week Harold Johnson spends nursing Otis's precious trees? The man hardly has time to do anything else. Of course his boot prints are going to be all over this orchard."

"Yes, I know Harold works hard. I also know he was steaming mad at Otis just a couple days ago, calling Otis crazy, so you might want to check on that. But about the prints, look closer, Gooder. These two prints aren't the same."

With an exasperated breath, the deputy knelt and stared at the print Jillian's finger hovered over. After a minute, he looked up at her. "They're the exact same size and same tread. What else is there to make them different?"

And he's been investigating crimes for fifteen years. "See that edge there? They aren't the same."

He rose to his feet. "Stay here a minute." He strode over to the technicians, who had lifted Otis's body onto a gurney, covering it with a sheet. After a few moments, he returned to her side. "There's no sign of blunt-force trauma or injuries not normally associated from a fall off a ladder. He was old, Jillian. He might have had a heart attack or just fainted and fell. Don't overcomplicate this." He nodded at the fruit trees surrounding them. "It's kind of poetic how Otis's life ended here, since he loved his peach trees more than any person."

A woman's shriek cut off their conversation. "Mr. Dupree! Mr. Dupree!"

They turned to see the housekeeper running toward Otis's body, items from her violently swinging grocery bags hitting the ground along her path. Finally dropping them altogether, she reached a hand down toward her longtime employer before rounding on Jillian. "He hasn't been the same since you visited him on Saturday." She jabbed a finger in Jillian's direction. "You killed him!"

The deputy slowly approached the distraught woman, speaking to her much more gently than he had to Jillian. "Mrs. Haines, the evidence, or lack of it, appears to indicate an accidental fall from that ladder."

"That don't mean she didn't drive him up that ladder in the first place." The woman's voice wavered. "It's all her fault."

He gently led the distraught woman away from the body and helped her pick up the fallen groceries. "To my knowledge, Otis no longer had any relatives left. Can you confirm that for me?"

Sniffling, the housekeeper shook her head. "Mr. Dupree was the last of a long, proud line." She dropped a cucumber into a bag. "What's this world coming to?"

As Gooder guided her toward the house, he gestured behind her to Jillian, mouthing what she took to say, *You can go.*

Jillian nodded and ducked out of the housekeeper's line of vision, but she wasn't yet ready to face Cornelia or Bertie.

As soon as the pair disappeared into the house, she walked to the far side of the property, taking a rambling route in the general direction of her car and trying to think calming thoughts, like the sermon she had heard the day before. *Peace. I could really use a little peace right now.* Her mind and body finally began to relax.

Until something dropped over her head and blinded her.

Jillian shrieked, trying to escape, but strong arms gripped her. Otis's murderer must have come back!

Jillian screamed again, just as the scratchy weight was removed from her head, and a familiar face materialized.

"Hunter?" she asked as her eyes stared into his concerned, handsome face. In his hands, he held a giant mass of Spanish moss. She looked up at the canopy of live oak branches that had dropped the giant bromeliad onto her head and slumped as the adrenaline drained from her body. "What are you doing here?" she asked before realizing what a silly question it was.

He tucked her hand into the crook of his elbow and guided her to a nearby stone bench. "The EMTs called me."

"I knew that," she muttered, swiping at her hair and blouse, sure there were bugs all over her. She hated bugs. She once watched a documentary with her former fiancé about people who had found bugs in indelicate places. She shivered and returned to shaking out her blouse.

"I figured you did," Hunter said politely and asked if she would like him to brush off her back.

"Oh, yes, thank you!" Jillian shifted on the bench, turning her back toward him.

His strong hands quickly skimmed along her back in a gentle sweeping motion. The random thought popped into her head that she was thankful Bertie wasn't around to witness this or she'd have the print shop churning out wedding invitations in the blink of an eye and Jasmine on standby to fix Jillian's hair for the big event.

"So what are *you* doing here again?" Hunter was asking her. "I thought you visited Otis on Saturday."

"I did. But even though he agreed to talk to me, he mostly spent the time taunting me about how he was not going to tell me anything." She flicked a dark speck off her slacks. "He did, however, devour the frosted cookies I brought from the bakery. If he'd known they were going to be his last, I wonder if he would have savored them."

Hunter's hands dropped from her back. "You're all clear."

"Thanks. Now I can drive home without being terrified of running off the road because a millipede is crawling onto my neck." She gazed out at the peaceful sweep of the grounds. "I had reason to hope he might be in a better mood today, so I thought I would try again. Now I might never know if Frederick Dupree really is buried at Belle Haven and what Otis might have known about it. Or why the two families that were once close drifted apart. Otis acted so strange. I can't help but think he knew at least some of the answers." She threw her hands in the air. "How can I solve this mystery now?"

Hunter glanced at her. "Would you like some help? I'd be happy to help you do some research or brainstorm the possibilities."

"Why would you do that?" Jillian couldn't help but ask.

"Well, I lived in Atlanta for many years, and Atlanta has historical markers about the war on almost every corner." His face turned sheepish. "And I might be a bit of a Civil War buff."

Jillian gave him a sideways look. "You're not one of those reenactment types, are you?"

His laugh was quiet but genuine. "No, I'm more of the poke-around-museums-and-read-books type. But over the years, I've developed a decent body of knowledge on the subject." He glanced over at the house. "I need to go now, but maybe we could meet tomorrow. How about three o'clock at the park?"

"The one where the farmers market is?" The open space was a little . . . well, open for her tastes. They'd be the focus of the gossip at the salon in two minutes flat. "It would make for a very quick walk, wouldn't it?"

"There are also some trails that start beyond the picnic tables," Hunter told her. "They aren't well marked, but the actual trails are kept clear."

Jillian felt a little foolish for not knowing that, but when one lives on ten acres of land, going to walking trails isn't usually necessary. "That sounds better. I'll see you tomorrow."

"Good." Hunter stood. "Stay away from the moss in my absence."

As he strode away, Jillian compulsively checked her clothes once more before climbing into her car.

By the time she pulled up to Belle Haven, she felt calm enough to face Bertie, Cornelia, and their questions. But she didn't appear calm apparently, because as soon as Cornelia looked up from her magazine and saw her, she said, "You've brushed against the veil today, haven't you?" She bustled her great-niece to a chair, insisting she sit while she poured her some tea before hurrying out of the room, shouting for her sister.

Sometimes Cornelia blew her mind.

A couple minutes later, she returned with Bertie in tow. "Here she is, Jillian. Now you can tell us what happened."

Jillian blinked at the sight of her grandmother. "I thought you'd still be at the shop."

Bertie waved off her granddaughter's surprise. "Savannah called about some paperwork she needed, so I came home to get it during the slow period. But what about you? Did you have an accident while you were on your errands?" Bertie asked. "You've kept your auto insurance current, haven't you?"

Her questions were practical, but Jillian knew they meant her grandmother was concerned, making her wonder what Cornelia had told her.

Jillian raised both hands to get her grandmother's attention.

"The car is fine, and I have not been in an accident." She lowered her hands into her lap. "But I went over to Dupree to talk to Otis about something in that journal of Bridgett Summerlin's I found in the attic, and . . . well, I found his body on the grounds." Even though she knew the two families had not been close for many decades, she still found it difficult to relate what had happened.

She saw Cornelia dart a glance at her twin before rushing to Jillian to hug her. "No matter how often we experience it, seeing a death is shocking. I'm so sorry, dear."

How many dead people did her great-aunt think Jillian had seen? "Actually, Cornelia, this is the first time I've stumbled onto a dead body." She hastened to add, "Not literally, in this case. It looked like Otis might have fallen off a ladder, but that's all I know so far."

"Of all the ridiculous things to do, climbing ladders at his age," Bertie said. Which was surprising, since Jillian had seen her grandmother perched on one on several occasions in the short time she'd been back. Although Bertie was far more limber than Otis, Jillian didn't think he could have been that much older than her grandmother.

Cornelia shot Bertie a sympathetic look. "Would you like some tea, Bertie?"

Jillian's mouth dropped open when her grandmother violently shook her head and fled the room. A moment later, she heard the door to Bertie's bedroom close none too gently. She turned to look at Cornelia. "Do you know why Bertie's so upset?"

But the woman who purposely scheduled her salon appointments for prime gossip time clammed right up. "I couldn't say, dear. Excuse me. I need to go find Raymond. He'll understand." She hustled out of the room in search of Possum, the cat who she was convinced somehow channeled the spirit of her dearly departed husband.

Left alone, Jillian sat gazing into her glass of tea, where an image of Otis's supine body floated on the surface. Shaking her head, she carried the glass to the sink and emptied the contents. Out in the yard, Cornelia was moving from flower bed to flower bed, searching for Possum. Jillian needed to get to the bakery, so after a quick stop by her bedroom to change into more suitable clothes, she headed for The Chocolate Shoppe. If working during the lunch rush didn't distract her, nothing would.

Although she said nothing to Lenora about what had happened, the older woman had some crazy-good observation skills and kept Jillian running from task to task, not leaving her a second to think of anything else—exactly what she wanted. A few of the customers thanked her for the sandwich bread sale. She couldn't think of an appropriate reply, so she quirked her mouth into something that approximated a smile and rang up their orders.

Once the pace slowed after lunch, Jillian turned her focus to replenishing the condiments and wiping down the tables. She glanced up at the sound of the shop door opening and saw Savannah enter.

"Hi," Jillian greeted her.

A look of concern spread across her friend's face. "Are you okay?"

Jillian tucked a collection of white, yellow, and blue packets of sweetener into a small tabletop dispenser. "It's that obvious?" Here she'd been thinking she was doing a good job of acting like it was a normal day.

"Yeah." Her friend dropped into the seat opposite her. "What's going on?"

"Can I get you anything first?" Jillian asked.

Savannah gazed at the baked goods display. "A half caff and a snickerdoodle muffin."

After she served the snack, she told Savannah what had happened at the Dupree mansion.

Her brown eyes wide behind her glasses, Savannah gave a low whistle. "What a horrible way to start your day. But a collective sigh of relief will be heard all over Moss Hollow when the news gets out."

"Ted Grady should be pleased, for sure," said Jillian, stuffing more napkins into the holder. Folks sure did plow through the paper products along with their pastries. "I wonder where he was at the time of Otis's death."

Savannah lowered her muffin to the plate. "Why? Did Otis's death look suspicious?"

"Gooder didn't seem to think so," Jillian admitted, "and there wasn't any physical evidence to the contrary." All things considered, she realized she'd gotten off light for someone who had discovered a body. "But at the risk of sounding like Cornelia, there's just *something* that seems off." She told Savannah about the different boot prints she'd found and pulled out her phone to bring up the photos.

Savannah stared at them as she chewed a bite of her muffin, then returned the phone to Jillian. "I don't know. I can't see much of a difference, but maybe the lighting messed it up."

"I think you would have noticed it, if you'd seen the actual prints," Jillian said. "You have a better eye for details than Gooder."

An eyebrow raised above the wire rim of Savannah's glasses. "For numbers, sure. But at death scenes, possible crime scenes? That's a bit of a stretch." She paused, staring out the storefront window. "You said something about Otis's time of death. Do you already know when he died?"

"Well, no," Jillian admitted. "But it seems logical that it happened while the housekeeper was shopping for groceries. Considering the size of the grocery in Moss Hollow, she couldn't have been gone very long." The memory of Dorothy Haines's accusation returned like a knife in her gut. "She told Gooder I killed Otis."

Savannah winced. "Ouch. Gooder didn't give you grief for it, I hope."

"No, not yet anyway. He thinks Otis's death was an accident. A simple case of a lame old man doing what he should have known better than to do. Falls from ladder. End of story." Jillian realized she was sounding a little bitter, but she couldn't shake the niggling suspicions at the back of her mind. "I'm going to ask Hunter if he'll tell me the time of death next time I see him." She left out the part about their planned walk at the park.

"Supposing you're right and it wasn't an accident, who would be a suspect? Obviously Ted Grady."

Jillian told her about the angry outburst she'd heard from Harold Johnson on her first visit to the Dupree mansion. "I forgot to tell you, but I didn't forget to tell Gooder. Not that he's likely to do anything with the information."

"If he doesn't, it's because he knows Harold much better than you," Savannah said gently. "Harold has had to develop a thick skin to work for Otis all these years. But deep down, he has a heart of gold." She shook her head. "He was just blowing off steam and trying to calm down. He would never let Otis know when the old man got to him."

Jillian's face fell. "Oh no. Are you sure?"

"Completely." Savannah popped the last morsel of muffin into her mouth.

"But we both know a certain someone that everyone in town said was the sweetest little thing, and you know how that turned out—"

"That was different. Some quiet types hold a world of anger inside, but Harold's a totally different personality. He lets off steam through outdoor stuff, like fishing and hunting."

"So he kills animals but not people is what you're saying." Jillian grinned.

Savannah wadded up her napkin with a chuckle. "Pretty much."

"Who else then?"

"Anyone Otis had business dealings with, and that's a good twenty percent of this town's adult population."

The shop door flew open, and Fanny Hughes burst inside. "You'll never guess what happened!"

With a quick glance at Savannah, Jillian said, "What?" She tried to sound neutral.

"Otis Dupree is dead!" the short, sturdy woman announced triumphantly.

Savannah offered a gasp that sounded pretty convincing, at least to Jillian.

"My husband saw the ambulance pulling out of the Dupree gate, so he went to the hospital to check on him. They said Otis wasn't there, so he must be dead!"

"His concern for Otis had nothing to do with your auction business, did it?" Savannah asked.

Fanny's round face darkened. "Of course not. What a horrible thing to say! But I know who did it, so save your judgment for the murderer."

"Murderer?" Savannah repeated. This time Jillian thought her gasp sounded more sincere.

"So they're calling it a murder now? That's the first I've heard of it. And who do you think did it?" Jillian pressed.

"Harold Johnson, of course," Fanny crowed, her anger gone. "Oh, and I need a cup of coffee and two of those delectable-looking muffins to go, dear."

Even in the face of Fanny's order, Jillian sat frozen. *So I'm not the only one who suspects Harold Johnson.*

Finally, Savannah broke the silence, rescuing her friend. "Harold worked for Otis for decades. If he was going to kill his employer, putting himself out of a job, wouldn't he have done it ages ago?"

"Just ask the waitress or bartender at Crazy Fish Bar & Grille," Fanny told them. "Lots of us heard Harold say he was gonna kill him."

"When did he say that?" Jillian asked.

"Saturday night." Fanny's phone rang, and she glanced at the screen. "I have to go. There's work to do."

As soon as the door was closed behind the woman, Jillian leaned over the table toward her friend. "So how's the food at Crazy Fish?" With Bertie and Cornelia always cooking, Jillian still had several local eateries to try.

"Their hush puppies and catfish are particularly tasty, but all the food is very good," said Savannah. "Would you care to join me for dinner after work? I need to get back to my accounts."

"How about six o'clock? I need to help Lenora for a few more hours to make up for the Saturday fiasco."

Savannah stood and tossed her napkin in the trash bin. "Perfect. It's out on the edge of town on Darby Creek Road. See you."

"Bye."

For the rest of the afternoon, Jillian maintained a hyper-focus on every task she did until Lenora asked if she had started taking some new miracle drug. Jillian assured her she had not.

"Well, child," Lenora said, "whatever you did earlier today, keep doing it, and we'll have us a real professional baker on our hands."

With a wan smile, Jillian took off her hairnet and prepared to leave. She'd have to find other methods of upping her baking skills, because finding a dead body every day would be counterproductive.

10

"Good thing I haven't washed the Prius yet," Jillian mumbled to herself as the car bounced through the thick dust of the red-dirt driveway of Crazy Fish Bar & Grille. The parking lot was nearly full, and it took a couple minutes for her to maneuver her small car into a narrow gap between two wide pickup trucks.

The building that housed the establishment was painted a periwinkle blue with green trim. Rainbow-painted wooden fish dotted the exterior walls. She opened the fuchsia door and entered the crowded main room. The blond hostess greeted her, and Jillian told her she was meeting a friend.

"Oh, your party is right over there, to the left of the picture window." The hostess pointed to a nearby booth.

Peering through the groups of diners, Jillian saw Savannah seated in a massive booth made completely of planks. She wove between the tables and dove into the seat across from her friend. "This is interesting already."

"Isn't it?" Savannah lifted her glass of red-tinted tea. "Try the raspberry tea. I usually don't like flavored teas anywhere else, but Crazy Fish does it right. It's particularly good with jalapeño hush puppies, which you should definitely try."

Jillian perused the colorful menu. "Whoever designed the menu knows what they're doing. The font choices are spot on. And the food looks good too."

"More importantly, everything tastes good as it looks. No gross, soggy nuggets tasting like old grease here." Savannah peered over the top of her menu. "I must confess that I've been known to occasionally pick up a meal to go, especially at the height of tax season. Sometimes it gets a little loud in here for me."

Jillian frowned. "If it's always so noisy in here, how could Fanny hear what Harold said on a Saturday night?"

"Good question." Savannah set her menu aside and looked around. "Fanny didn't say what time she was here, right? Only that it was night?"

"Uh-huh. It could have been six or nine or eleven." The sign by the entrance door listed the weekend closing time as midnight.

A waitress in a Crazy Fish T-shirt and bangs the color of the restaurant's front door approached their table. "I see your friend found us, Savannah. Hi, I'm Amber. What can I get you to drink?"

"I hear the raspberry tea is good, so I'll try that," said Jillian. "But from what Savannah has told me, I could order anything and it would be good."

"Pretty much." Amber grinned. "Malcolm, the owner, says people have been asking if they can buy a franchise of the place. He says there's no duplicating it, and he's not lying."

Jillian liked this girl with the cheerful bangs and neatly painted blue fingernails. "Do you work weekends or only weekdays?"

"I'm usually off Sundays and Wednesdays, unless someone calls in sick on those days. But Fridays and Saturdays are totally off-the-hook fun."

Savannah smiled wide. "You might know a friend of ours then. Harold Johnson? He was here Saturday night."

"Oh, Harold! That poor man." Amber's bright bangs skimmed her forehead as she shook her head. "The first time I waited on him, he kind of scared me. I figured he'd be cranky and stiff me on tips, but I was so wrong. There was this one day when I had a flat tire."

Jillian imagined the waitress had them regularly, given the rough entrance to the parking lot.

Amber continued, "Harold saw it and changed it for me. Then left me a nice tip." The waitress paused and leaned closer to Jillian and Savannah. "But he was having a hard night on Saturday."

"I'm sorry to hear that," said Jillian. "What happened?"

Amber lowered her voice. "Well, you know who he works for, right?"

The two women nodded.

"Not an easy job," Savannah said.

"I know, right?" Amber looked relieved. "The old man must have been extra cranky because Harold was letting off a lot of steam at high volume right there in the middle of the dining room." She pointed a short blue fingernail to the exact spot. "After a few beers, he started telling everybody that he'd be happy to never see that old buzzard ever again."

"Those were his exact words?" Jillian asked with a little laugh, attempting to downplay how important the answer was to her.

"Yep. Harold usually says things like that when he's had a hard day. He's said it so often we all just nod in sympathy because we know he's just blowing off that pent-up frustration that comes from working for a mean old coot like Otis. Harold's really a stand-up guy." The waitress looked over her shoulder. "Malcolm's giving me the eye over there. I'd better take your order."

After telling Amber what they wanted, she hurried away, leaving them to let off a little steam themselves. "Fanny's memory was a bit off, wasn't it?" Jillian immediately said. "'Gonna kill him' is way different from 'happy to never see him again.'"

"I told you Harold wouldn't do it. He's a crusty knight with a tire iron, not a vengeful murderer." Savannah sat back in the booth. "If Fanny keeps passing her version around town, Harold's going to end up as a suspect."

"And I didn't help, telling Gooder about what Harold said to me." Jillian sighed. "Maybe I should pay Harold a visit and see if

I can find out anything to counter Fanny's gossip. I hope he has a good alibi."

"And I hope there will be no need for him to have one. But it sounds like a good plan, anyway."

"I promised Lenora I'd work the early shift since I did so well today, which means I didn't burn anything or mess up any dough or batter. I'll visit Gooder when I'm done."

Savannah nodded toward the kitchen. Amber was heading their way with a plate of appetizers. "You have a busy day tomorrow, so eat up."

After wrestling with a queasy stomach most of the day, Jillian suddenly felt famished.

The next day, as Jillian was settling into her car to drive to Harold's home, Albert returned her call. She almost ignored it, as she did not recognize the number displayed and didn't want to end up fielding impertinent questions from some random sales company. At the last second, she sighed and accepted the call, and was thankful she did.

"Miss Green, this is Albert. I apologize for the delay in calling you back. I was out of town all day yesterday on a project."

Jillian rolled down her window to let air into the car. "I understand, Albert. As I mentioned in my message, my grandmother, great-aunt, and I would like to talk to you about doing a few projects around Belle Haven. Could you come tomorrow morning at ten o'clock?"

Albert paused, apparently looking at his schedule. "I can be there. I'll bring some examples of my work."

"We'd appreciate seeing them," she told him. "See you then." With the tension of Otis's death weighing on her, Jillian was relieved to be taking steps to give her family's home some of the care it badly needed. It gave her a small sense of being in control. Of something, at least. She just hoped the cost wouldn't put the work out of financial reach. Annalise had recommended Albert highly, but as the wife of a bank vice president, her pockets were probably deeper than theirs. But Jillian would worry about that tomorrow.

Returning her attention to the immediate task ahead, she headed away from town, toward Harold's property. The neat lawns and gardens disappeared, replaced with wild flowers, untrimmed trees wearing vines like skirts, and goldenrod swaying with native grass. She hoped the GPS on her phone didn't get her lost, or she could end up in the wrong state before realizing it.

"In one quarter mile, turn left," the computerized voice commanded.

"Yes, ma'am." Jillian switched on her signal.

She drove past ponds and abandoned barns, finally seeing a rustic but neatly kept wooden fence. Just in the nick of time, she saw a sign hanging on a metal gate: Johnson's Camp. She made a hard right, her tires flinging dirt and stones, stopping the car within a few inches of the closed gate.

"Your destination is on the right."

"Wow, thanks." Jillian climbed out of the car and examined the gate. She was beginning to wonder if her plan to visit unannounced had been a wise one. There was a heavy chain wound through the gate and fence, but she realized it wasn't secured with a lock. Glancing around her, Jillian unwound the chain and walked the gate open enough for her car to pass.

Pulling the car through, she jumped out again to close the gate behind her. *This would get really old, really fast.* The driveway meandered through thickets and fields, finally leading her to several buildings—a three-sided shed, a small bunkhouse, and a larger cabin with porches at both ends.

She parked between the two houses, peering around for any attack dogs before opening the car door. Just in case, she pulled a can of wasp spray from her purse. Lenora had told her it worked twice as fast as pepper spray and would stop anything from a wasp to an unreasonable man. Jillian hoped she'd never have to test the validity of those claims.

As soon as her feet hit the dirt, the barking started. Jillian was about to jump back in the car when she heard a shout and the barking stopped. Harold strode around the corner of the larger house, a camouflage hat on his head and a pipe hanging from the corner of his mouth. It bobbed as he yelled to her, "Who are you, opening my gate and helping yourself to my property?" Two dogs, one the size of a small horse and one low to the ground, tagged behind him.

The fingers holding the spray can shook."Harold, I'm Jillian Green. I'm Bertie Harper's granddaughter, and I live at Belle Haven."

Closer to her now, Harold took the pipe out of his mouth and pointed it at her. "I've seen you before. You were at Dupree's last week. Funny thing, Otis went from bad to worse after that day." The pipe went back in his mouth. "What are you doing here?"

At least he hadn't accused her of killing Otis *outright* like the housekeeper had. "I'm sorry I surprised you like this, but I wanted to talk with you privately. About Otis's death."

Harold's eyes had a natural droop, giving him a sad bloodhound look. At the mention of his employer's death, they drooped a little more. "I suppose you do. Let's sit down."

He waved her over to the porch of the cabin, where three well-worn yet sturdy rocking chairs sat. A line from Bridgett's journal came to mind in which she'd mentioned that her aunt

Olivia had reminded her, "Young ladies should avoid rockers." Well, at thirty-nine years old, Jillian could hardly claim to be a young lady, so it was all good.

"Have you heard any details about Otis's death?" Jillian sat in the rocker closest to the steps.

Harold slid off his hat and rubbed a hand over his scalp. "Some. Enough. Only matters he's gone now."

The depth of sorrow in his voice surprised her. "I understand you've worked wonders with the Dupree home and grounds for decades. You created something very special there. I'm sorry about what happened."

The man nodded but didn't reply.

"I know you don't need the details, but it appears that some people in town do because some gossip is spreading. Sorry to say, it's about you."

Harold snapped his head sideways to stare at her. "So? Gossip doesn't matter. Only truth."

"It would be nice if that were so. But you were heard saying angry words against Otis at Crazy Fish, and I'd hate to see you become a suspect in his death."

"A suspect? The fool man went and climbed a ladder I spent half a lung tellin' him to stay off. How can an accident have a suspect? And if there *was* a suspect, wouldn't it be you?" So he had heard that detail too.

She chose to ignore the last part. "All I know is that someone came into my family's bakery and started telling us that you had killed Otis." The horse dog padded over to her, bumping against her leg. She reached down and ran her fingers slowly along the rich, carmelized brown of his spine. "I don't think you killed Otis, or I wouldn't have come out here alone. I'm not completely clueless. And I'd like to be able to give the gossipers something factual to silence the accusations. Do you have an alibi I can share?"

Harold shuffled to his feet. "Come with me and I'll show you."

Jillian knew deep down it was safe to go with Harold, but she still felt it best not to let her guard down completely. "How about I follow you?"

"Fine." He stepped into the cabin, returning a minute later to hold out a scrap of paper. "Here's the address. In case we get separated. Should take you 'bout ten minutes." He whistled to his dogs, and they followed him to his truck.

Before she started her car, she quickly texted Savannah to let her know where she was going, just in case. Then she followed Harold down his long driveway and out onto the road. She was trying so hard not to lose sight of the truck that she didn't notice where they were heading until Harold pulled over against a curb and parked. After stopping behind the truck, she looked up.

Harold was standing at the door of Big Bud's Taxidermy Shop.

11

Harold held the door open for her, waiting.

Jillian gulped, feeling like her feet were welded to the sidewalk. She'd never understood the fascination with taxidermy, but it seemed to run rampant in the state of her birth.

"You coming or not?" Harold asked, tucking his pipe in the pocket of his brown shirt.

With a shrug of surrender, Jillian walked past him into the shop. Glass eyes of all shapes, sizes, and colors stared at her. Claws, teeth, tusks, and antlers seemed to cover every possible inch of wall space. Jillian cut to the chase so she could escape. "So, this is where you were on Saturday morning? Is there some security footage we can use to prove it?" There could be a security camera in each staring eye, for all she knew, which was the only reason she could think of why anyone would hang a head or body on their wall.

"No, we didn't get back here till late afternoon, after you found him."

"Oh. Then why are we here?" Maybe he was less of a crusty knight than she thought.

"Sure are an impatient little thing, ain't you?"

Maybe she had inherited something from Bertie after all. "I come by it naturally."

"Follow me."

The last time she had followed him, she had ended up here, which did not encourage her to do it again. "Um . . ."

"They can't hurt you anymore, you know." Was it her imagination, or was there a glint of humor in Harold's eyes?

"No, but they're doing a pretty good job of creeping me out." She shuffled her feet forward. "Let's get this over with."

She tried to comfort herself with the thought that maybe the next room had pretty things in it like preserved wild flowers. But her imagination quickly ran wild again. *Or maybe it holds more reptiles than one can find in all the waterways in the county, including the occasional pool.* Jillian clamped her mouth shut before the whimper got out.

There were no flowers or snakes to be found in the next room. Just a man bent over a table, using tweezers to perform some delicate procedure on a fish.

Fish?

"How's the crappie coming along, Bud?" Harold asked.

"Almost done. Then I can start work on the trophy of the season." Bud grinned and set the tweezers on a tray of instruments resembling a dentist's collection of torture tools.

"This is Jillian. Can she see our catch and the video?"

The expression on Bud's face as he looked her up and down sent a blush spreading over hers, and she wondered how many women Harold had brought there. *Ew.* No wonder he was still single. "I'm only here to help Harold with some gossip. That's all."

Bud looked confused, so Harold gave him a quick summary, which in his style took about five words.

"Really? Huh. People are strange," Bud said when Harold finished. "Well, at least you've got one beauty of an alibi." He led them out the back door to a separate building, which contained a walk-in refrigerator and freezer. Unlocking the refrigerator, he shoved the door open. "You can stay out here, if you don't want to freeze," he told Jillian. "Give me a hand, Harold."

The two men disappeared for a couple minutes, and then Jillian heard the sound of wheels on the concrete floor. A giant gator snout lurched out at her, easily big enough to swallow her. She jumped back with a muffled yelp.

"Ain't he a beaut?" Harold beamed at her.

"He's certainly impressive," she said. The beast was so big that he was stretched over four industrial carts. "But he doesn't look like he can speak on your behalf, Harold."

"Don't be too sure about that." He lovingly patted the gator's massive knobby head. "Hold on while we put him back and I'll show you."

A few minutes later, she was seated next to Harold in front of a large-screen computer while a mounted white-tailed deer appeared to watch from its perch over her head. She stared straight ahead at the screen's camouflage background.

Bud used a computer mouse to select and open a file. "This is footage from when Harold bagged the gator on Monday. The time stamp runs along the bottom."

"Did Otis normally give you Mondays off, Harold?" Jillian was curious.

He rubbed the stubble on his chin. "No. But gator season was ending on the fifth, so I asked for a long weekend. It's not like I don't work plenty of weekends for him." He frowned. "I mean, didn't." He waved at the computer. "Come on, start it."

Jillian began watching her first—and hopefully last—gator hunt. The beginning time stamp was quite early, early enough that Harold could have made it back to Dupree had the hunt been quick. But it went on. As fascinating as it was to watch Harold sitting in a blind by a lake and making lady gator noises in an attempt to draw the male gator his way, the whole thing made Jillian uncomfortable. After a few minutes, Jillian held up a hand. "Um, Bud, could you please skip forward through some of this? In five-minute intervals would help."

Bud exchanged an amused look at Harold. "Sure."

Even during the shortened version, she kept wanting to wave the gator away, as it eventually followed the imitation sound to its doom. But there was no denying Harold had a kind of courage she couldn't fathom, the kind that stayed cool when the huge beast's maw opened and snapped an inch from Harold's booted feet. That's when he'd shot the beast to finish him off.

It was probably not a story she was going to share when she refuted the gossip that Harold had killed Otis. While the time stamp made it clear Harold was nowhere near the Dupree mansion on Monday, it did show him to be unflinching at taking a life, even if that life was a twelve-foot reptile.

Harold removed his hat, toying with it. "I was right proud of this take. He was a wily one. But now he'll always be the reason I wasn't there to save Otis's life. Like I said, I'd been telling the old man to stay off the ladders for years. Why didn't he listen?"

Bud quietly closed the video file.

Harold turned to Jillian. "I'm going to have a gator feast in memory of Otis. I'm going to tell everyone about the man only I really saw. You're welcome to come. There'll be plenty."

"I'd like that," she heard herself answer. "Thanks for the invitation. When will it be?"

"Can't rightly say yet," said Harold. "I'll let you know when I can."

Jillian struggled her way out of the deep-set couch, imagining the deer head laughing at her. "I have to go now. If I hear anyone spreading tales about you, I'll be sure to set them straight."

Harold nodded his thanks, setting his cap back on his head.

Turning to the taxidermist, she said, "Bud, thanks for your help. Your shop is something else."

Bud grinned. "Thank you. Come back any time."

Not unless somebody's life depends on it, Jillian thought as she walked out under the gauntlet of glass eyes.

By the time Jillian was prepared to leave for the park to meet Hunter, with Bridgett's journal tucked in her backpack, the visions of glass eyes swimming before hers had mostly retreated into her subconscious. Since the backpack was designed to protect laptops, she supposed it would protect the old leather book well enough. She doubted the trails in the small community park were very rugged. By timing her departure at a time when Bertie was at the shop and Cornelia had already left for a meeting of the Moss Hollow Garden Club, Jillian had managed to avoid uncomfortable questions, such as "Where are you off to this time, Jillian?" and "Oh, you're meeting Mr. Greyson? I'll call the chapel as soon as you give me a date." Only Possum remained in the spacious home, and he was too busy grooming himself to pay her any mind as she left the house.

The cool morning had warmed to an almost uncomfortable temperature, but at least the humidity had remained lower than it had been all summer. Jillian had swept back her hair into a ponytail to keep the frizz from attacking as she walked. Pulling into the small parking area, she saw Hunter leaning against his dark silver Lexus under the shade of a line of trees bordering the far side of the field where the market was held. She parked beside the Lexus and climbed out of the car, backpack in hand.

Hunter straightened as she approached. "Hi, Jillian. You look ready for a ten-mile hike."

She realized he was looking at her backpack—and that she was seeing him in shorts for the first time. He definitely didn't fit her idea of a mortician. "If you're expecting tasty trail mix and such, you'll be sorry to hear this is for Bridgett's journal. I'd feel horrible if, after a century and a half, it came to harm because I tripped on a walking trail. So I figured this would be good protection."

Hunter's blue eyes crinkled at the corners as he smiled. "Smart thinking. About halfway through the loop trail, there's a bench that would make a good place to stop and look at the journal."

"Sounds perfect." The last thing she needed was gossip tearing through town that she'd been seen snuggling with the handsome mortician in the park, which is exactly how it would be interpreted if anyone saw them looking at the journal together.

"The trailhead is over there." Hunter pointed to a small wooden walker's gate set between two towering trees.

She felt better about not noticing it before. It was difficult to see in the shade. The small crooked entry was designed to keep motorized vehicles off the trail, so they passed through it single file and then walked side by side as the path widened. The area bordering the path featured a simple, understated beauty compared to the designed, manicured grounds of several antebellum mansions in the area, but Jillian delighted in its contrast. During her years in California, she'd forgotten the unique habitats that mingled in her home state. She supposed she'd always taken them for granted.

"I'm glad you suggested this trail," she said. "I like it."

"I'm told it was built about seven years ago," Hunter told her. "Part of the county's rails-to-trails program."

"Ah, the town meetings over that change were lively, I'm sure." Jillian applauded the citizens who had championed the cause, or the peaceful trail might have been bulldozed and turned into one of those ugly strip malls. She wondered if Bertie or Cornelia had participated in the discussions.

"I was still in Atlanta so I missed it, but I suspect you're right." Hunter leaned down to grab a large branch laying on the trail. "Are you still recovering from yesterday's events?"

Jillian gave a somber laugh. "Recovering might not be the right word, but I've had no shortage of distractions." She told him about her visit earlier in the day to see Harold and about accompanying him to the taxidermy shop. "And to think I used to hold the firm belief that Moss Hollow was a boring place. How wrong I was. It's a crazy quilt of characters."

"I have to admit, my work since moving here from Atlanta has changed dramatically," Hunter said. He gave her a smiling glance. "But the scenery is nice."

Jillian waited for a witty response to occur to her, but nothing came short of an urge to blush, and she'd already done enough blushing for one day. She blurted, "So, do you know the time of death for Otis?"

He showed no sign of being startled by the shift in conversation. "Even though I'm the county coroner, I don't have the equipment to do the detailed exams, so I can't give an exact time. But just from years of experience, I'd guess it was not much more than a couple hours before you found him, give or take thirty minutes."

"Two hours. That definitely clears any doubt of Harold being involved. The video clearly showed Harold sitting in the hunting blind making those ridiculous gator noises well before then. And that was only the start of his day." Jillian was relieved for Harold but still couldn't shake the feeling that Otis's death was more than a simple, unfortunate slip. "I'd ask Dorothy if she'd seen or heard anything suspicious before Otis's death, but she's too busy blaming me. I seem to have that effect on people."

Hunter's arm snaked out and plucked a low-hanging branch right before Jillian was about to walk into it. "And here I haven't yet accused you of a single death." He grinned. "In my line of work, that's saying something."

"Give it time," Jillian quipped. "You've only known me a few months. Speaking of your work, has anyone contacted you to make arrangements for the funeral?"

"No, but there was no need. Otis prepaid for his funeral long before I moved here, leaving detailed information about what he wanted. The visitation's on Saturday."

"I'll tell Bertie and Cornelia, though they may already know by the time I get home." Jillian pointed to a generous-sized bench overlooking a pond. "You're right, that's perfect." They sat down, and Jillian pulled out the journal, glad to see there was plenty of room to hold the leather journal between them.

"Wow, that's an impressive journal for the period." He examined the lock and leather binding with reverence. "It's not quite like any I've seen."

Jillian showed Hunter the dedication page. "This is why."

"A homemade present worth treasuring for sure," he said after reading Bridgett's notation. "Sounds like she had a good relationship with her brother."

A leaf drifted down from an overhanging tree to land softly on the page. Jillian brushed it off carefully. "The cultural differences from today were startling for me, even after studying the period several times in school. I always thought people back then rarely traveled, mostly sticking close to home except for the rare trip. But Bridgett's family seemed to always be visiting one relative or another, as well as friends, for days, weeks, or even months at a time. Yet the Summerlins sound like a very close and loving family. It contradicts what I've seen in plenty of movies about the Antebellum Period and the Civil War."

Hunter nodded. "I've noticed the same thing in some of the collections of letters from plantation families I've read too. Obviously, it was those families who had the funds to travel so often, but they also maintained an amazing volume of correspondence with extended families and friends."

"It did pave the way for plenty of free lodging." Jillian turned to another page. "Here's another example of a homemade gift." She read aloud: "'Mother sent me an exquisite gift along with her last letter, the most precious frame woven with her own hair. Inside was a miniature of Mother and Father. Mother sent it to keep me from missing them overmuch.'"

"Did you find the miniature too?" Hunter asked.

Jillian shook her head. "I didn't read about it until later. Although it might be worth poking around."

"It would be a unique family heirloom if it held up through the years as well as the journal did."

"'There's something else I'll look for that you might appreciate." Jillian turned to the later part of the journal. "Bridgett also received what she called a 'beautiful little perfume casket.'"

Hunter laughed. "Sounds kind of creepy, doesn't it?"

"Just a little." Jillian's eyes lit up, and she turned to the next page. "Bridgett's next entry might interest you. She's invited to a dinner in honor of a couple from Atlanta. Savannah said the names sounded familiar, but she couldn't remember why." She shifted the book so Hunter could read the entry.

With his head bent over, Jillian had a nice view of the way a slight curl had sprung up against his neck in the warm afternoon air.

"Oh." Hunter sounded surprised as he lifted his head.

"What?"

"I do know something about the couple. Cyrena and Amherst Stone." His brow furrowed in thought.

She tried a more insistent tone. "*What?*"

"Well, from accounts I've read in several sources, the Stones were secret Yankees. Especially Cyrena. As an attorney and businessman, Amherst's loyalties apparently wavered at times. But their emotional—and most likely some financial—support went to Union soldiers."

Jillian blurted, "Yankees? Why would Bridgett, a member of my family tree, be socializing with Yankees?"

"You don't suppose . . . ?"

Jillian finished for him. "My family line could have harbored secret Yankees."

Jillian hunched over the journal again, studying the entry. "The dinner invitation was given by a Mary Stansel. Does that sound familiar at all?"

"No," said Hunter. "I don't remember reading anything about that family. Their connection with Atlanta may be through family members with a different last name. You'd have to research the Stansel family tree."

"Look." Jillian tapped a finger on a single line. "Bridgett mentions speaking to Frederick, but there's no indication of Jedediah being there. She was fond of Jed. Surely she would have recorded his presence if he had attended." She frowned. "I remember Bridgett writing about her mother warning her to be extremely judicious when choosing with whom to socialize. And considering the Belles were a planter family whose livelihood depended upon labor-intensive crops—vastly different from a lawyer or merchant family—I'm convinced Vernon and Olive were not 'secret Yankees.'"

"Can't argue with that logic," Hunter said with a hint of admiration. "And it's entirely possible that neither they nor Bridgett's family had any inkling the Stansels were Union sympathizers. Many of them were experts at covert support, like women baking money into pies and slipping them to Union prisoners held in Atlanta."

"Bertie would be horrified. A foreign item in baked goods? Perish the thought!" Jillian was relieved to know she wouldn't have to break the news to her grandmother and great-aunt. "I'm puzzled about Bridgett, though. I didn't see anything in what she wrote indicating she had become a secret Yankee, before or after her visit to the Stansels. It feels like I'm watching a TV series that gets canceled after a cliffhanger season finale."

As she finished her sentence, a slow grin was already spreading across Hunter's face. "Ah, but vee haf vays," he said.

Jillian giggled. "You sound like a bad actor trying to play Dracula. You should be careful about that, given your profession. But continue."

With a rueful shrug, Hunter dropped the accent. "You know how early Christians used to indicate their faith to other believers by drawing an ichthus?"

She nodded. "I did attend vacation Bible school when I was a child."

"Secret Yankees used similar methods. They'd display a symbol in plain sight because it had a generic cultural meaning that would be overlooked as anything special."

"What about the handmade hair frame Mrs. Summerlin sent?"

"I'd have to see it and check for an inscription on the back to be sure, but I doubt it." Hunter leaned back, stretching an arm along the back of the bench. "Examples I know of are specific quotes from Shakespeare, displayed as needlework or calligraphy, or Bible verses, or lines of poems or ancient dramas like *The Odyssey*. Well-to-do families were generally committed to emphasizing classical culture in the raising of their children and in decorating their homes."

"An uncultured woman lacks beauty," Jillian said softly. "One of Bridgett's grandmothers sent her a reminder of that in a letter. Bridgett mentioned it in her journal."

"Great example," said Hunter. "Have you seen anything like what I mentioned around Belle Haven?"

"I didn't know to look for them so I can't remember. But I'll poke around some." And the simple renovations she had discussed with Bertie and Cornelia would give her the perfect excuse for snooping. Having a game plan flooded her with renewed energy. "Thanks, Hunter. You've been a big help."

"And you gave me a chance to use an interesting hobby for a good cause." He ran a finger along the outline of the journal's lock. "Seeing this was a real treat. Original period sources don't turn up very often these days." He stood. "Shall we finish the trail?"

Jillian nodded, carefully placing the book inside the backpack. "And to think I owe the discovery of this journal to Possum." Cornelia would get a kick out of that.

After finishing the loop of trail, Jillian and Hunter parted before the after-work exercisers arrived, much to Jillian's relief. As she drove home, her phone lit up with a call. It was from Belle Haven.

She answered, "Whoever this is, I'll be home in five minutes."

"I hope not," Cornelia responded. "We have a crisis in the kitchen and need your help."

"Crisis?" Jillian asked. "What now?" She thought of Bertie's odd behavior on the morning Otis died. "Is Bertie okay?"

"She did seem a bit under the weather. Maybe that was why she came home early," Cornelia said. "But we've got bigger fish to fry. We've run out of shortening, and I need it for dinner. Please stop by the grocers and pick some up."

Knowing Cornelia, Jillian figured there would be fried chicken, not fish, for dinner. Again. "For you, I'll make a U-turn," she said.

"I knew you could help. I'll make the biscuits while I wait."

"Bye, Aunt Cornelia."

One U-turn and a short drive later, Jillian entered the grocery store and heard a clatter of gossip as she made her way to the correct aisle. People greeted each other with "Did you hear where Otis fell?" or "Do you think he had help?" and one "I heard it was Harold Johnson that done it!"

No time like the present to start nipping that in the bud, Jillian thought. She turned to the man who had suggested that Harold had been involved in Otis's death. "Maybe you should ask Big Bud where Harold was when Otis died."

She grabbed the largest can of shortening on the shelf—it would last at least a couple of weeks—then hurried to the express checkout line and set the blue container on the belt. The owner, Wit Doyle, scanned the can. "Cornelia frying chicken?"

"How'd you know?"

"Only time a Belle Haven woman buys one item."

He was probably right since the family had shopped there a good many years. "You definitely have your finger on the pulse of Moss Hollow's cooks, Mr. Doyle."

He grinned. "Part of the job."

Jillian paused for a moment. "You know, I can't help but think about another cook, Dorothy Haines. What with all the talk going around. It must be weird for her to know Otis fell while she was here shopping."

"Oddly enough, Dorothy's usually like clockwork with her grocery run, but she was running late last time, tearing up and down the aisles like a house afire. Had to get out the floor buffer to take out all the skid marks."

"Sometimes life is just unpredictable," Jillian said casually, handing the man exact change.

"Sure is." Mr. Doyle took the money and gave her a receipt. "Enjoy that chicken."

"Thank you. I'm sure we will." Jillian exited the store thinking about Dorothy.

Why had the woman been running late that day? What had she been doing earlier, like when Otis died? Jillian had a hard time picturing Dorothy offing her employer after witnessing her reaction to seeing his body, but stranger things had happened in the short time Jillian has been in Moss Hollow. It would be a while before she'd have the time, but Jillian thought a conversation with the housekeeper was in short order.

She just hoped Dorothy didn't have any more verbal jabs to throw her way this time.

Jillian chewed her bottom lip as Lenora inspected the rows of cupcakes she'd decorated. To her eyes, the treats looked uniform and enticing, two important qualities in baked goods. But Lenora was the toughest customer she'd face all day.

The woman finally gave a quick nod. "Take them to the case." When she disappeared into the refrigerator, Jillian allowed herself a single fist pump before carrying the heavy tray out front. She'd made it almost to the end of her early shift without a single mishap. Not even a tiny one.

The bakery's front door opened, and Harold Johnson ambled in, looking almost surprised to find himself in such an establishment.

"Hi, Harold. Can I interest you in a cupcake or three? Fresh as they come."

"Those things are too froufrou for me. I like something with more substance." He padded along the display case like he was sneaking up on a wild turkey before jerking a thumb at the glass. "Two of those. And black coffee."

Jillian slipped two apple fritters into a bag and filled a coffee cup. "Anything else for you?"

"You can come to the gator feast tonight. Six o'clock, my place." He took some bills from his duct-taped wallet and held them out to her. "There's plenty, so you can bring someone if you want."

Jillian handed him some coins. "Thanks, Harold. I'll be there."

With a nod, he took his fritters and coffee, and left, whistling.

"You should take that nice undertaker," Lenora said behind her.

Jillian jumped, accidentally slamming the register drawer

shut with her hip. "*Ow.* You have even more stealth powers than Bertie." She rubbed the tender spot. "I'll bet the kids in your house never got away with anything when you were around."

"You know it, girl." Lenora walked over to the bread display. "So are you going to make the call or not?"

Jillian pulled her phone from her pocket and sat down at a bistro table. Selecting a contact, she held the phone to her ear while Lenora made miniscule shifts to the positions of different breads.

"Hey, Savannah. How would you like to experience a gator feast with me at Harold Johnson's tonight?" She heard Lenora snort behind her before returning to the kitchen.

"I've heard Harold knows how to do a gator feast right," said Savannah. "What time?"

"Six."

"Sure. I'll pick you up at five thirty. I'm glad it starts before sunset. It's black as death out there at night."

Jillian shuddered. "It was hard enough to find the place in broad daylight." She glanced at the clock on the wall. "I'd better run. Josi's brother is coming to the house at ten."

"Good. I hope it goes well."

"Me too. But if we decide to hire him, all three of us will have to agree on what to have him tackle first."

Savannah chuckled. "Sounds like fun. I'll see you later."

By nine fifty-five, Jillian had changed out of her bakery clothes and was watching Cornelia place a final brownie on a china plate. A tray holding a pitcher of tea and glasses rested nearby. "Are you trying to feed Albert enough to keep him on a sugar high for the entire renovation?"

"Never negotiate with a man with an empty stomach. It makes them hard to get along with." Cornelia straightened up. "There. We're ready."

"Isn't he here yet?" Bertie marched into the room. "We can't hire someone who doesn't know how to read a clock."

"It's not quite ten. Don't go on the warpath just yet." Cornelia paused in front of the mirror, making little adjustments to her bangs. The doorbell sounded. She turned to check the clock. "See? Right on time."

Bertie harrumphed as Jillian walked away to answer the door.

When she returned with Albert beside her, the two sisters stood at opposite ends of the sofa. "Albert, this is my grandmother, Bertie, and her sister, Cornelia."

"Ladies, it's nice to meet you." Albert's deep voice sounded foreign in the room, which was always occupied with females. "You have a spectacular home." His admiring eyes traveled around the room. "Amazing workmanship."

"Thank you, Albert," said Cornelia, waving a hand at the mound of brownies. "Please, sit down. Would you like a little something to eat before we get started?" She reminded Jillian of a model on television game show.

Albert sat in an armchair opposite the sofa. "My sister tells me your desserts are the best in town, so I don't think I can refuse."

Cornelia piled two large treats onto a china plate and served it to him along with a glass of tea. "How kind of her to say so. We are so pleased to have Josi in our little group on Sundays."

Jillian could have sworn she saw a glint in her great-aunt's eye when Albert took a substantial bite of brownie. Maybe she was calculating how much the cost of the projects had just lowered.

The three women watched him eat while they sipped their tea, although Jillian tried to be less obvious about it. To his credit, Albert didn't seem to be intimidated by the scrutiny.

After he finished, Albert set the plate, empty now but for a few crumbs, on the coffee table. Opening his briefcase, he took out an electronic tablet. "I brought a slide presentation of some of the historical projects I've completed." He offered the tablet to Jillian.

Jillian sat between Bertie and Cornelia so they could all view his photos. She was impressed by Albert's thorough preparation. Bertie and Cornelia leaned in close as a parade of homes and buildings filled the screen, each tagged with the duration of the project and the specifics of the work done. After the final mansion faded from view, the screen filled with a list of Albert's skills, certifications, and license numbers. Jillian felt better about the thought of putting the renovations in Albert's hands, if they could find the budget for it.

She returned the tablet to Albert. "I see why Annalise recommends you so highly."

Albert nodded, offering a crooked smile. He looked at the two sisters. "Do you have any questions?"

Bertie shifted away from Jillian to return to her end of the sofa. "Josi told us you were a general contractor for many years. Have you kept your hands-on skills up to date? We can't have someone with rusty skills working on our family home."

Albert leaned forward in his chair. "I enjoyed my years as a contractor, but I never stopped using the craftsmanship I'd developed. I didn't want to only use my brain and computer. My electrical skills and certifications are up-to-date and top-notch, as well as heating and air conditioning."

"Plumbing?" Jillian asked, thinking about all the strange noises she heard when she used the second-floor bathtub.

"I'm currently in the process of recertification on that," Albert answered. "It will be completed in about a month."

Pity.

Cornelia looked at Jillian and her sister. "Why don't we take Albert on a tour of the house? Let him see everything and tell us what he thinks are the most important projects to do first. Then we can discuss all the information and decide."

"Good idea," said Jillian. "What do you say, Bertie?"

"I say what are we waiting for?" Bertie stood, causing Albert to spring to his feet. "We don't need to bother with the kitchen, since we've always kept it in good repair."

Albert walked to the nearest window. "Updating windows can be a very cost-effective repair, often saving the owner enough on their heating and cooling bills to cover the cost over time. May I?"

They all nodded, watching as he opened and shut each window and tested the panes and weather stripping. Then they all moved on through the rest of first floor, the women observing how Albert studied, touched, and listened to each room before continuing to the next one.

Forty-five minutes later, they all returned to the living room. Albert proposed that they begin by replacing the windows and updating the wiring on the first floor to avoid fires. The other floors could be done at a later time.

"Your suggestions are very helpful," said Jillian. "Would you mind waiting on the veranda while we discuss things, Albert?"

"Oh, and do take some more of the brownies," Cornelia said sweetly.

As soon as he left the room, the fun began.

"It makes sense to begin with the foundational things like the wiring," said Jillian. "When I plugged in my phone charger last week, there were sparks."

Bertie nodded. "And he's right about the windows. They don't hold out the elements like they used to."

"But those things are no fun," Cornelia complained.

"We could redo the library," Jillian suggested. "Try and make it less creepy."

"Oh, no. If we start hosting events here, we'll make a bundle with the library," argued Cornelia. "People will pay good money to experience the psychic movement in there."

"Enough, Cornelia. There is no psychic movement in the library—or anywhere else for that matter," Bertie said firmly. "An office with some good lighting, however, would be helpful."

Jillian had taken a corner of the desk in her room for a makeshift office, but it was difficult to get much accomplished there. "Would it be for all of us?"

"I don't see why not," Bertie answered. "There are plenty of good-sized rooms to choose from, and we could each have a desk with lighting, some cabinets."

"I think I know what we could use for the cabinets, and it would be very inexpensive." Jillian shared her idea of refinishing and adding shelves to the tack cabinet.

"What a great idea," Cornelia said. "It's both practical and creative. Let's do it."

Together they went out to the veranda to speak with Albert. He stood looking out over the gardens. They explained what they wanted, and he agreed to prepare a written estimate for the projects.

"I'll email it to you by the end of the day tomorrow," Albert said.

"Don't feel like you need to rush," Bertie cautioned.

Cornelia nodded. "Yes, take your time."

"I'll be thorough and accurate—don't worry."

"Oh, we're quite sure you will be," Cornelia said. "I just thought I'd use the time to prepare Raymond for having another man around the house."

Albert looked confused. "Josi told me you were both widows. Is Raymond your son?"

"Never mind that." Bertie shot her sister a barbed look. "Tomorrow evening would be fine. Jillian checks her email quite often, so send it to her. We'll go from there."

After Albert had disappeared down the road toward town, Jillian decided it was a good time to pay Gooder a visit. So when Bertie left to drive to The Chocolate Shoppe, she dropped Jillian off in front of the sheriff's office.

Laura Lee Zane was leaning over the reception desk, talking with the secretary, when Jillian stepped into the room. She approached the young female deputy but remained quiet until Laura Lee and the dispatcher finished their conversation.

The dispatcher attended an incoming phone call, and Laura Lee turned away from the desk. "Good to see you, Jillian. I heard about everything you went through on Monday. You okay?"

"Thank you, yes. I guess everyone in Moss Hollow has heard about it by now."

Behind them, the dispatcher spoke into her headset, "No, ma'am, the sheriff's office cannot issue any restraining order, whether it's on your neighbor's ceramic gnomes or trying to force your neighbor to remove them from his lawn. You'll have to get the municipal judge to agree to that, and I doubt if he will."

After the two women shared a subdued laugh, Jillian continued. "I'm doing a lot better than Otis, but I did want to speak with Gooder. Is he here?"

"He'll be grabbing lunch soon, but you caught him in time," Laura Lee answered. "He's in his office."

"Great. It shouldn't take long." Jillian hurried down the hall and rapped on the closed door. She heard the groan of Gooder's swivel chair before the door opened.

The deputy sighed. "I was just leaving for lunch, Jillian."

"Don't worry, I won't keep you long." Jillian entered Gooder's closet-sized office and sat on the edge of the visitor's chair, which brought her knees to the point of almost touching the deputy's hefty desk. "Do you have any new information on Otis's case?"

Gooder blinked at her like an owl. "What case? Otis Dupree died when he fell from a ladder." He pointed to piles of papers on his desk. "Does it look like I need to spend time on something that clearly doesn't impact public safety?"

"But did you see the coroner's report?" Jillian figured if she threw enough questions at him, he'd finally give her some information so he could go eat.

"I talked briefly with Hunter Greyson. And as I already told you, the fall is what caused Otis's death. Good ol' gravity. There was no conclusive evidence pointing to any other cause."

"Nothing conclusive?" Jillian pounced on the word like Possum on a vole. "By any chance does your non-conclusive evidence point to Dorothy Haines?"

Gooder slammed a fist down on the metal desk. "*Nothing conclusive.* What part of that don't you understand? And why would you even ask about Dorothy?"

"Because I found out she was not at the grocery store until shortly before she returned to the Dupree estate, and she shopped really fast. So this begs the question: Where was she during the time when Otis was killed?"

"Stop saying he was killed." The deputy's jaw tightened.

"But you can't deny that she had the opportunity to harm him." Jillian wrinkled her nose. "And just being around Otis for so many years probably gives her a plausible motive."

"You know who else had opportunity?" Gooder stood and leaned over his desk toward her. "You!" His face softened a bit. "Look, Jillian. You found Otis dead, and it was a traumatic experience. I think your mind is looking for a way to deal with that. To process what you saw. Maybe an appointment with your pastor would help. Now, I'm going to lunch." He straightened and opened the door, holding it for her. "Go find something fun to do. Get your mind off what happened to Otis."

His words jolted her. Snapping her mouth shut, she exited the tiny office without another word. When she passed through the reception area, Laura Lee was nowhere in sight. Just as well. After Jillian's encounter with Gooder, she had some thinking to do.

14

Jillian marched down the sidewalk, her frustration fueling her speed. Gooder Jones saw her as a traumatized woman with delusions. *What does he know about my tolerance for handling stressful situations?* Finding Otis's body had been a shock. That she couldn't deny. But she'd borne up well under extremely stressful situations in the past, like discovering her fiancé was a crook, losing the career she'd spent years building because of it, and having to move across the country to start over—all in the matter of a few weeks. Sure, none of those things had involved finding a dead body. But they had been traumatizing for her, and so far she hadn't cracked.

She quickly said a silent prayer of thanks.

From across the street came the sound of church bells, first counting out the twelve strokes of noon and then playing a song. The music calmed her thoughts, and she realized how futile her anger was. If Gooder was right and no one had had a hand in Otis's death, then nagging the deputy would never bear any fruit. But if she wanted to find out if her suspicions were right, she needed to do everything she could to find out the truth.

By the time Savannah stopped by Belle Haven to pick up Jillian for Harold's feast, Jillian's mood had completely changed. The two women went along the country roads with the windows down, singing songs from their high school years. After a rousing version of "Shine," Jillian remembered how Gooder had suggested she do something fun, and here she was, following his advice. But he never had to know it.

Savannah drove down the long driveway and parked next to the three-sided shed alongside several trucks and Jeeps. Two long picnic tables sat under strings of lights hung between two towering loblolly pines. "I didn't realize there would be so many people here."

"Harold said there was going to be plenty of food, but I didn't expect this," Jillian confessed. "I'm doubly glad you agreed to come." She saw a familiar figure appear from the shed, carrying a pot as big as any found in The Chocolate Shoppe's professional kitchen. "There's Big Bud, the taxidermist. You have to meet him."

"I've heard of Big Bud. He sounds like quite a character," Savannah said. "I'm surprised you didn't scream like a banshee when you were in his shop."

"Thinking about it now, what Bud does isn't that different from Hunter's profession," said Jillian. "Hunter just doesn't suspend his clients from the ceiling when he's finished."

Savannah swatted Jillian's shoulder, wrinkling her nose. "Well, there goes my appetite. Thanks so much."

Jillian pointed at the outbuilding. "There's Harold. I guess we better stop gabbing and join the party. Maybe we'll hear something about Otis that will help us figure out how he died."

"Harold probably knew Otis better than anyone except his mother and Dorothy." Savannah opened the driver's-side door. "I think this is going to be one dinner I'll never forget."

A tall, thin girl with fuchsia bangs walked out of the barn carrying two large bowls. "Hey, look. It's Amber from Crazy Fish. At least there's one person here that we know a little." Jillian waved to the waitress.

"She managed to find a way to still serve on her night off. We should see how we can help too." Savannah's initial shyness dropped away.

Amber grinned at Jillian's wave. "You two are having some mighty fine eating this week."

"Remind me of that when my slacks don't fit next week," Jillian said as she and Savannah caught up to the waitress. "Is there anything we can help with?"

Amber nodded toward the building. "Malcolm's back there organizing everything. Ask him and he'll put you to work. Most of the guys are in there, but they're sampling the dishes when Mal's back is turned. Harold's out by the fryer. Once the gator nuggets are done, we need to eat as soon as possible. That's the best way to enjoy them." She started moving toward the tables, and Jillian and Savannah went to the outbuilding.

"I've never seen a kitchen in a shed like this," Jillian said.

"They're pretty common, and they're handy," Savannah told her. "It makes a big difference in the summers. You don't have to heat up your whole house cooking inside. Here, you have the air circulation but enough cover to keep the sun off. Plus, you don't have watery chili if a storm kicks up."

As they entered the shed, they saw Malcolm bent over, taking huge pans out of a double oven. He placed them on a stainless steel work area next to the appliance and turned around. "Please tell me you're not here to sample the dinner menu. We have enough people filling that role." Four men hovered nearby, and Jillian could almost hear them salivating.

Jillian laughed. "No, we asked Amber if we could help, and she sent us in here to ask you."

"Good. You can take these to the tables. Two pans each. The serving spoons and pot holders are hanging over there." He nodded at the large metal rack suspended over the workspace. As Jillian and Savannah moved over to grab what they needed, he called out, "And thanks."

The aroma rising from the pan gave Jillian some sympathy for the four men who were trying to snag the job as taste testers. Whatever was in those pans smelled amazing.

"Have I thanked you enough for inviting me?" Savannah bent over her pan and inhaled deeply.

"Considering Lenora suggested I ask Hunter, probably not," Jillian joked. The pan smelled wonderful, but it was heavy so she picked up her stride.

Savannah's mouth opened into an *O*. "I wasn't a spite invite, was I? Because why would you invite me over the gorgeous undertaker?"

"I already knew I was going to invite you. We've eaten two meals together already this week. Why not go for a third?" Jillian walked to a nearby table and set the pan down. "I'm kidding. Hunter's helped me with the Civil War information, but you've been the one making sense of Otis's death, so it never occurred to me to invite anyone else."

Savannah's pan balanced out Jillian's at the other end of the table. "Thanks. I feel better now." The two women went back for the second pair of pans. They had delivered those when Harold came around the corner of the building, carrying a huge platter, its contents covered with a checkered cloth. A man and woman trailed him, each with a platter identical to his.

Jillian smiled when she recognized the man with Harold. "Hi, Big Bud!" she greeted him. "This is my friend, Savannah."

"And this is my wife, Cammie," Bud said, grinning and turning to the woman beside him. "Married twenty-eight years, and she's still as pretty as the day we wed."

Cammie was only an inch or so shorter than her husband, with a head covered in tight brown curls cascading to her shoulders. Jillian couldn't help but wonder how they looked at the height of the summer's humidity. With or without frizz, Bud's wife was a looker.

Her smile was wide and friendly. "Bud told me about your visit to the shop. It sounded very similar to the first time he took me to a taxidermy shop—on a date, mind you—to show me what he wanted to quit his insurance job to create." She broke into a hearty laugh, and her husband chuckled alongside her. "I had some wild dreams during the weeks leading up to our wedding, I can tell you. But I got used to it."

"Are y'all going to get those gator bites to the tables or stand there jawing?" Harold scowled at his friends, but his eyes told a different story. They quickly distributed their platters among the tables, and Harold yelled toward the house. "Moonie, where's the tail? Make it snappy!"

Ten minutes later, twelve people were seated at tables laden with so much food, Jillian wondered if the legs would hold. Wilted dandelion salad, hush puppies, and the alligator served three ways: gator bites, steamed tail with drawn butter, and aromatic gator mac and cheese. Harold told the seated guests that he would save the talking for dessert, a fitting peach cobbler, to which the four men from the barn whooped.

Jillian and Savannah learned their names were Jimmy, Nate, Trip, and Wayne. Moonie, who had been in the main cabin steaming the gator tail, sat next to Malcolm, a man who looked to be in his sixties with a dimpled chin and a bright-white mane of hair. Jillian was beginning to think Harold picked his friends to balance out his own lack of hair on top of his head.

Harold stood and motioned for everyone to suspend the chatter. "Thank you for coming to my gator feast in honor of the only employer I've ever had. May he rest in peace, 'cause he didn't have much himself while he was living. But he gave me my livelihood and allowed me to improve this property my pop bought when I was a little squirt."

"You're still a little squirt!" a mountain of a man jovially shouted.

Harold pointed at the man. "Wayne, you keep on interrupting, and you can enjoy your gator cold." The man harrumphed but kept quiet. "Anyway, thanks to the folks who helped cook and stuff. I'm going to fill up for a bit, then I'll share some memories I have of Otis. Now eat up, everyone!"

Jillian looked at her plate, trying to decide what to try first. Figuring the steamed gator tail would cool off the quickest, she tentatively inserted her fork into the hunk of meat, surprised when a tender piece fell right away from the rest. She gave the forkful a quick dip into the ramekin of melted butter by her plate and put it in her mouth.

When she finished the bite, she leaned over to Savannah. "After tasting that, I have more empathy for the guys who were begging to be the early tasters. I've never tasted gator before, but this is pretty good."

Savannah nodded. "I've eaten gator, but never so tender. The gator bites are amazing too. The dipping sauce is delicious, but you don't really need it."

Amber leaned across the table toward them. "That's why Harold asked Moonie to cook the tail. It takes someone who really knows gator tail and knows the exact moment to take it off the heat so it's not rubbery or dry. Moonie's the best in the county at steaming tail. Malcolm told Harold that while he'd make the mac and cheese, Moonie was the one to ask to steam it."

Jillian noticed there was little chatter for a group of twelve people. She followed suit and turned her attention back to the meal. Beside her, Savannah did the same, clearly enjoying her plate of food. But like Jillian, her eyes were actively taking in her surroundings.

Everyone was still reveling in the flavors and textures on the plates when Harold put his fork down and started sharing some of his memories of Otis, pulling his pipe from his pocket and fiddling with it as he talked.

"I was fifteen and scrawnier than a stray dog." He scowled at Wayne to discourage any interruption. "Even though Pop had worked for Otis for a good twenty years by then, there was no real reason for Otis to take a chance on hiring me as an assistant." Harold shook his head. "Especially since I'd been getting into a little trouble now and then for a couple years."

Moonie nudged Nate, a young man who sat beside him. "Sounds like someone else we know."

Jillian saw the round-faced youth blush.

Harold continued. "Then, after Pop trained me about the trees and what needed to be done, Otis finally gave me what I thought was an important job. He told Pop to have me burn a pile of brush that had built up. The boss was trusting me with fire on his property."

The chewing stopped.

Harold stared up at the loblolly branches looming over the tables. "I'd built fires for camping plenty of times. I guess I got a little careless and a wind kicked up that caught me slacking. Before I realized what was happening, the fire was licking at the outer row of peach trees."

Jillian winced at the thought of those beautiful fruit trees burning. She heard Savannah draw in a hushed gasp.

"By the time Pop and I, and even Otis, got the fire turned and under control, a good fifty trees were charred and dead." Harold's grip on his pipe tightened, and Jillian hoped it was made from sturdy lumber. "I waited for the police to come and arrest me for destruction of his property, but no one ever came to take me away. The next day, I stayed in bed, knowing Otis wouldn't want me around Dupree ever again. Then Pop came in and yelled at me for not being ready to leave for work." Harold leaned over for his glass and took a long draught, as though the fire from so many years ago was still stuck in his throat.

Jillian looked over at Savannah and mouthed, *Wow*. Her friend's eyes were wide as she nodded her agreement.

"Mind you, it was another decade before Otis trusted me with a fire again." Harold laughed, and his friends joined in.

The next story related how his father's illness one year had led to them being late to spray the trees to protect them from the plum curculio, a dreaded pest. Harold explained that they only have a few days to spray and had missed most of them, so Otis had himself donned coveralls and helped spray the trees.

Jillian had a hard time conjuring a picture of Otis in coveralls. Harold had been right when he said he would tell them about an Otis only he knew.

After spinning a few more tales running the gamut from humorous to emotional, Harold took a break and served the peach cobbler, apologizing for using frozen fruit because the season for peaches was over. Jillian couldn't tell the difference and scraped the delicious remains from her plate, astonished she was able to eat it all after such a large feast. She felt more stuffed than any animal Big Bud had worked his taxidermy magic on.

As the guests began to move away from the table and mingle, Harold approached Jillian and Savannah. "What do you think about Otis now?"

"He definitely had facets to him that I never would have imagined," she answered. "I haven't heard of a single person in town with those kinds of positive memories. If they have them, they're certainly not out there sharing them. Thank you for tonight."

The sun had set, and the twinkle lights suspended over them cast tiny spotlights over the man's face. "I forgot to mention that Otis paid for Pop's funeral too. So when the old man got grouchy or unreasonable—yeah, I'd let off some steam. But I always remembered what Otis had done for me and Pop. The job was bigger than me."

"Harold," Savannah asked quietly, "what do you plan to do, now that Otis is gone?"

The man was silent for a moment before answering. "Otis's attorney asked me to stay on for a while to maintain the grounds while the estate is settled. That's all I know. After that, well, I'm thinking of working for myself. Would be nice for a change."

"Will we see you muttering 'The boss is crazy!' then?" Jillian grinned.

Harold barked out a laugh. "Wouldn't bet against it."

Jillian's face grew sober. "Harold, how well do you know Dorothy? Is she capable, in your opinion, of losing her patience and hurting Otis?"

Harold's face was still, then he shook his head.

Jillian told him how she'd learned that Dorothy didn't have an alibi for the time of Otis's death as she had led them to believe.

After a deep sigh, the man reached behind his neck and untied a leather choker, handing it to her.

Jillian stared down at the large tooth attached to the cord. "Is this . . ."

"From my first big gator kill. Show this to Dorothy, and she'll give you her alibi."

Jillian had heard of secret handshakes and code words, but a tooth? "Thanks, I think. I'll be sure to get this back to you." She surely didn't want it in her possession any longer than it needed to be. "Savannah and I are going to head for home, but thank you again." She slipped the choker into her pocket. "This has been enlightening and very enjoyable."

"Keep a watch for deer on your way back," Harold warned Savannah. "A big buck would crush the side of that little thing you drive." He turned back to Jillian. "If you want my opinion, you'd be spending your time better finding out where Ted Grady was on the morning Otis died."

Jillian nodded. "Thanks for the tip." She and Savannah waved good-bye to the lingering guests and made their way back to the car, using their cell phones for light.

"So how are you going to find out what Ted was doing the morning Otis died?" Savannah asked on the way back to Belle Haven.

"I'm not sure yet. Still thinking on it."

"I'll try to think of something too, but in my business, if I ask about other people, folks get antsy and think my lips are too loose to do their books."

"You can't jeopardize your business. And I haven't a clue what to ask anyway. Maybe Bridgett will show me in a dream," Jillian joked. "That seems to work for Aunt Cornelia sometimes."

Another early morning shift at the bakery had Jillian concerned she might actually become a morning person. *Enough of that silly notion,* she thought as she drove along the long driveway back to the Dupree mansion. She thought of the stories Harold had shared last night. They took the horrid experience of finding Otis's body and added poignancy to it. Jillian found it oddly comforting, or maybe the shock was finally starting to dissipate.

When Dorothy saw Jillian at the open door, her eyes narrowed. "Now what do you want?" she asked none too graciously. But at least she wasn't screaming about Jillian being a murderer. *Progress, not perfection, right?*

"I just need to talk with you for a minute, Dorothy," Jillian told her. "I need to ask you something."

Dorothy shook her head and started to close the door.

"Wait! I know you weren't at the grocery store when Otis died. Mr. Doyle told me." She hoped the significance sunk in for Dorothy quickly before she was left standing outside. "Where were you?"

The housekeeper's mouth tightened, and she again shook her head.

Jillian pulled the gator tooth from her jeans pocket and held it out in front of Dorothy. The housekeeper stared at it for a long time, and then her shoulders slumped. Stepping back, she opened the door wide. "Come in."

Dorothy led her to a bright, pleasant sitting room on the opposite side of the house from Otis's study. The sofa was considerably more comfortable than the horsehair one at Belle Haven. At least, Jillian didn't think it would give a person a rash if they sat on it in shorts.

"I don't know why you think you need to keep asking questions about that morning, when the sheriff's office says Mr. Dupree's death was an accident," the housekeeper said, still standing. "Why can't you just let this go?"

"Because something about Otis's so-called 'accidental death' just doesn't ring true to me." Jillian leaned forward. "Harold told me you were not capable of hurting Otis. And I do have a level of trust that Harold is telling the truth."

"You got that right," Dorothy said. "Harold Johnson doesn't have a lying bone in his body. So why aren't you taking his word for it when it comes to me?"

"Two reasons. First, someone taught me to trust but verify when I was younger. I ignored the advice not long ago, and it brought me nothing but grief, so now I try to have trust but also verify everything. Second, like with Harold, if I know why you weren't here—why you couldn't have been here and caused Otis's death—I can, with clear conscience, counter anything I hear to the contrary. You know how a small town is."

Dorothy's eyes flashed. "What gives you the right to be telling people about where I was in the first place? And checking up on me with Mr. Doyle? Who are you, some kind of female Geraldo Rivera?"

"I didn't mean I'd give details," Jillian said. "If anyone around Moss Hollow starts to say that you might be involved, I could simply and freely state that the speculation is not true and that my sources are verified and protected. That's it. Nothing more."

Jillian watched Dorothy's eyes transition slowly from an icy stare to something more vulnerable. Dorothy slowly lowered herself into a blue-and-white-striped armchair. "When you have the struggles I've had, trust is mighty hard to come by. But I'll try." She looked out the window for a moment before facing Jillian. "I've been a recovering alcoholic for years. AA meetings have been a regular commitment I keep to protect my sobriety. Lately, I've run into a tough patch, and I don't mean with Otis. So I met my sponsor before going to the grocery. That's all." Her hands twisted together in her lap. "Maybe Mr. Dupree would still be alive today if I hadn't been so weak."

Jillian's heart ached for the woman. Here she was trying to battle a pernicious addiction, and she had come home to find her employer dead. "Dorothy," she said gently, "you were out of the house for your usual amount of time. Whether you were on one errand or two, it wouldn't have changed the outcome. Otis still would have been dead. Don't carry a burden that isn't yours."

Dorothy swiped at her eyes with the back of a hand. "You're right. I'd forgotten about that. With my past, I'm used to being the one to blame, and rightly so. This is different."

"It sounds like you've been working very hard to build a new life." It struck Jillian how Otis had hired two people with admitted issues and kept them on his staff for years. The knowledge was messing with her long-term view of his character. He definitely was someone who freely tossed his weight around, but apparently there was another side to him.

"You know, if Harold hadn't given you that fool necklace of his, I'd never have told you anything. Not after the way Mr. Dupree reacted that day you first came here."

"How was it different? I mean, how did he react with other people?" Jillian asked, puzzled. As far as she knew, Otis had treated her as she imagined he usually did any of his visitors.

"With most folks, he didn't go tearing around the house, frantically searching the whole place."

Jillian didn't expect that answer. "Do you know what he was looking for?"

"I do, but it makes no sense to me. Maybe it will to you." Dorothy left the room for a couple minutes, returning to place a framed piece of needlework in Jillian's hands.

Jillian read the two lines, stitched in navy thread:

The arms are fair,
When the intent of bearing them is just.

Jillian was confused as she read the words. Where had she heard those words before? Why was Otis so agitated by her visit that he ransacked his home until he found it? She flipped the frame over. On the paper covering was the inscription *For Frederick, 1861.* Her pulse began to quicken. Here was a connection to Frederick Dupree and the year of his death.

Jillian tried to act as nonchalant as she possibly could. "Do you have any idea who this Frederick might be? Did Otis give any indication that he knew who it was?"

"He said nothing to me about it, but that is no great surprise." Dorothy gave a small shrug. "As I said, it makes no sense to me for a grown man to tear around a house looking for some needlework. Then he told me to get rid of it!"

"Why didn't you?" Jillian could have jumped up and hugged the woman right where she stood, but she kept up her calm, cool front.

"Well, it's an antique, if the date on the back is true. And it's a finely done piece. I do handwork myself. I just couldn't bring myself to destroy it. So I hid it in my room. I told Mr. Dupree I'd taken care of it. That wasn't exactly a lie. I did take care of it."

"It's definitely an antique. You were right to save it." Jillian set the piece on the sofa beside her. "Is it okay if I take some photos of it?"

"Sure, but you can have it, if you want," Dorothy told her. "Since Mr. Dupree didn't want it anymore, I think that would be all right."

Jillian considered the offer, then shook her head. "I think it's best for you to keep it, Dorothy. The photo will work fine for my purposes of research." She took snapshots of both sides of the piece with her phone and returned the frame to the housekeeper. "Thanks. Did Otis have any other visitors in the week before his death?"

"No, no visitors. I did hear him yelling into the phone, but that was fairly common."

Jillian hoped she wasn't pushing too hard, but she had to try. "Were you able to hear any of what he was yelling?"

Dorothy ran a finger over the framed words. "Not much. Mr. Dupree always told me to steer clear when he was on the phone." She smiled slyly. "Of course, sometimes I had to be cleaning close by. Other times he would holler so loud that I didn't have to be close. That day, I heard him say something about a woman at the bank. A Sheila . . . Shawna . . . No, it was Shelly. That's it, Shelly. But that's when I knocked a brass bookend off the shelf I was dusting because I wasn't paying attention. He shut right up so I couldn't hear any more."

Shelly. A woman at the bank. Jillian didn't know a Shelly in Moss Hollow, and she certainly didn't know anyone at the bank. But she knew someone who would: Annalise Reed, fellow Sweetie Pie and the wife of the bank's vice president. She stood. "Thanks, Dorothy. I really appreciate you trusting me with all of this. I promise no one else will need to know where you were that day. I won't betray your trust."

Nodding, Dorothy walked her to the door. No longer having Otis to tend to, her life was going to change dramatically, as was Harold's. Jillian hoped she'd find a new supportive place of employment. She parted, telling Dorothy she'd see her at the visitation Saturday.

Before she drove home, she pulled out her phone and looked at the photograph of the needlework. *The arms are fair, when the intent of bearing them is just.* What secret was hidden within those embroidered words that Otis had been so eager to destroy?

Driving home, she wondered if there might be a similar wall hanging somewhere in Belle Haven. She couldn't recall anything like it, but she probably wouldn't have made a connection before. The words would have had little meaning for her before. *I don't really know what they mean even now,* she thought. *Somehow the quote has some connection with Frederick Dupree, but what?* With all the excess space in the rambling old house, there were many rooms Jillian had barely been in. Today, with her work completed so early in the day and with Bertie at the shop, it would be the perfect time to do some snooping.

Jillian didn't expect to find any indication that Vernon and Olive Belle were Union sympathizers, but spending the day exploring might also turn up some other furniture pieces she and Savannah could refurbish for sprucing up the main parts of the house. After the last few days, she was ready for a little alone time anyway.

When she entered the living room, Cornelia was curled up on the sofa, reading a magazine aloud to Possum, who was also curled up next to her. Her great-aunt paused to greet her. "Hello, dear. Would you like to join Raymond and me? I'm reading a story from *Beyond the Realms*, although he doesn't seem as interested in it as I am."

There was a time when Jillian would have assumed a title like that would indicate a story in the fantasy genre, but that was before she had become reacquainted with her great-aunt.

"Thanks, but the renovation plans have inspired me, and there's something I want to work on today." She gave Cornelia an abbreviated, but somewhat evasive, explanation. Then, with a hug, she started for the stairs before she could get caught up into more conversation.

"Remember to listen to what the rooms have to tell you, Jillian," Cornelia called after her. "Listen and consider."

"Sure, Aunt Cornelia. I'll try." Jillian's room had had little to say to her in the months she'd stayed in it, as far as she could tell. She doubted the other rooms would get chatty either.

Inside her room, Jillian spent a little time reading Bridgett's journal. She wanted to start in the rooms that were most likely to have been Bridgett's during her visit. One of the earlier entries Jillian had read the night she and Savannah had found the journal mentioned Bridgett's room being on the second floor. Jillian's room definitely did not have any embroidered wall hanging with the mysterious words anywhere, so she considered the other rooms. One was Cornelia's, then another on Cornelia's side of the floor. The room next to Jillian's was the one that Cornelia had once told her had "a strong psychic vibe." The last one had once served as a game room.

Since Cornelia was currently occupied, Jillian tiptoed around the landing to her bedroom, squelching her uncomfortable feeling at the intrusion. But she'd told her aunt she'd be poking around upstairs and had not received any negative response.

She entered the comfortable bedroom, examining the walls as quickly as possible, then ducking into the shallow closet in case there was something hanging inside. Jillian wasn't surprised not to find anything since she was sure Cornelia had redecorated her room when she moved in. Most likely, she would have stored any unwanted items in the attic. Jillian darted out of the room, relieved to be back on the landing.

Jillian laughed inwardly, thinking of how she would have felt had she needed to look around Bertie's bedroom. She wasn't sure she would have dared, but she would never know since her grandmother's master suite was located where the servants' quarters used to be and, therefore, shouldn't house anything related to Bridgett's journal. *I can live with that.*

For the rest of the rooms, she took a more leisurely pace, allowing herself to appreciate the workmanship and creativity the architectural details represented. She thought of the look in Albert's eyes when he talked about his work in historical homes. Although she didn't find any framed embroidery, other than a beautiful design of a magnolia, she did find a lowboy she thought would benefit from a good refurbishing. She took a couple of photos from different angles to send to Savannah.

Padding around to the other side of the landing, she came to the "psychic vibe" room. She'd not felt the pull to go into this room. Maybe the vibe Cornelia had felt was Bridgett's, and she'd left a gift for the people who would come after her. Or maybe Jillian had been listening to her great-aunt a little too much.

Opening the glass-knobbed door, the first thing Jillian did was sneeze. The next time she saw Cornelia heading toward the room, Jillian might suggest she take a dust rag with her. She went to the tall window across the room and opened the curtains to let the light stream inside. The dust motes danced in the sunshine. Even though there was no evidence that this was the room Bridgett had stayed in, Jillian found herself picturing the young woman sitting at the slim desk by the window, writing letters to her family and friends, and pouring her soul into the leather journal her brother had crafted for her. But still, Jillian didn't find what she was looking for, not on the walls nor inside the large armoire.

Maybe she was wrong and Bridgett had never supported the Union. Perhaps she had attended the dinner at the Stansels' home, unaware of their sympathies. But the exploration was not a total waste of time. Jillian thought the armoire would be a stunning piece to use after a little tender attention.

Back in her room, Jillian opened her laptop and opened her Internet browser. She still had a nagging recollection of the saying that was embroidered on the wall hanging in the Dupree mansion. She opened the photograph she had taken on her cell phone, and typed the words in a search engine:

The arms are fair, when the intent of bearing them is just.

What popped up on the screen surprised Jillian. The words came from Shakespeare's *Henry IV*. Jillian's mind rocketed back to her meeting in the park with Hunter. He had said that underground groups, such as Union sympathizers or so-called "secret Yankees," often used a common quote as an identifier to let one another know of their political or religious leanings. Someone in the Dupree household had embroidered this passage from Shakespeare and had dedicated it, "For Frederick." A memorial to a young man on a star-crossed, Union-inspired mission. Somewhere around Moss Hollow there just might be an echoing message from others in the movement. *And maybe it's right here in Belle Haven.*

Next Jillian emailed the photos of the furniture she'd found to Savannah. While in her email application, she took a moment to check her own and saw one from Rosenschein Restorations. She glanced at the time, impressed at the promptness with which Albert had sent the estimate for the proposed work. She opened the email, hoping the amount wouldn't cause heart palpitations for either Bertie or Cornelia.

Staring at the numbers, she wasn't sure how to react. On the one hand, the estimate was fair, especially for work on an historic building. On the other hand, the reasonable amount for only a small portion of the needed renovations was still high enough to make Jillian wonder how she and her family could ever afford to truly keep up with improvements Belle Haven would continue to need over the years. It made her brain hurt.

After dinner, Jillian shared the information from Albert, figuring she'd let Bertie and Cornelia enjoy their meal before ruining their appetites. She also read some positive reviews she had found online at a Renovation Reviews website. "I have some money in savings," she added. "I can pitch in on some of the cost."

Bertie stared down at the numbers on the paper Jillian had given them. "I can't say it's highway robbery, but it'll take a chunk out anyway." She looked over at Cornelia. "What do you say, Sister?"

Cornelia reached down to Possum, who had plopped himself on top of her feet, and ran a hand along the soft fur of his back. "We need to take the plunge and trust all will be provided. We have enough for a start between us, don't we?"

Jillian and Bertie admitted they did.

"Then call the man, and let's get started." The decision made, the atmosphere in the breakfast room lightened. What they were proposing to do looked impossible to Jillian, but Bertie had kept her massive family home running for decades through sheer force of will, and she obviously wasn't about to give up now. And neither would Jillian.

At Bertie's direction, Jillian called Albert to inform him of her family's decision. Surprising her, he asked if they minded if he got started the next morning. Holding a hand over the microphone, Jillian asked Bertie and Cornelia what they thought and they both approved. When she relayed their response, Albert responded, "I'll be there at nine o'clock."

When Jillian ended the call, Bertie announced she would be taking a day off from the bakery and Jillian would need to be there until closing. After her grandmother left the room, Jillian grinned at Cornelia. "Bertie may be taking a day off from the shop, but she won't be sipping mint juleps on the veranda."

"No," Cornelia agreed. "Bertie will be following that man so closely, she'll almost be in front of him. I hope he realizes what he's getting into."

Jillian laughed. "I hope he doesn't, or he'll surely be a no-show."

16

True to her word, the next morning, Bertie shooed Jillian from the house immediately after breakfast, staying behind with Cornelia and Possum. At first, she felt disappointment at missing the start of the renovation, but the longer she thought about it, the more Jillian realized her grandmother had done her a favor.

Ever since she'd found Bridgett's journal, Jillian had been digging into Belle Haven's past and felt anxious about its future. At the bakery, she was forced to stay firmly in the present or culinary disaster could happen. On this day, the bakery was exactly where Jillian needed to be.

But that didn't mean she wasn't anxious to get home once she and Lenora closed up shop. Jillian was tired, but not too tired to listen to all the details of Albert's first day. What impressed her most was the fact that he planned on returning again the next day, even though it was Saturday. Even Bertie's intense supervision hadn't run him off the job.

"Of course, the lunch we served him should help compensate for the most annoying labor conditions," Cornelia had said when she told Jillian about how Bertie had managed to find some reason to be in or near the neglected room they had selected as the new office. "I'm sure Josi is a good cook, but it's always nice to eat something different sometimes."

"Like how I've gone from eating salads and grilled chicken breast to potato salad and fried chicken?" Jillian said.

Cornelia beamed. "Exactly, dear. All that grilling isn't good for a body. I hear it causes cancer." Her great-aunt had a point, all right. A deep-fried one.

When Bertie entered the kitchen, Jillian asked her if she planned to stay home for another day to help Albert. "How could I possibly help the man, Jillian? He's a professional."

Jillian willed her face to stay passive. "When do you want me to work tomorrow?"

"If you can take the early shift, I'll come after lunch and help Lenora close."

"That works for me." She really had changed, seeing an early shift as positive when she used to barely be able to drag herself into the corporate offices by nine o'clock in California. Now she'd have a chance to observe Albert in action. But she'd make sure to stay out of his way. "We're all going to Otis's visitation at six, aren't we?"

"Of course," her grandmother said brusquely. "Make sure you're ready on time." Cornelia reached over to pat her sister's shoulder but was shrugged off. Bertie bid them good night and left the room.

Jillian was beginning to think the most interesting person to watch during the memorial service was going to be her own grandmother. And she had no idea why.

Early the next morning, Jillian made the drive to The Chocolate Shoppe with her windows down. The air had a heaviness to it, and she wondered if they were in for a thunderstorm. Thankfully, the folks of Moss Hollow didn't let a little thing like rain or wind keep them from their coffee and bear claws on a Saturday morning.

When she walked through the back door into the kitchen, Lenora was already working on the bread and the mixers' bread hooks were whirring. "Morning, Lenora. What do you want me to do first?" She fit a pink hairnet over her ponytail and donned a white apron.

Lenora's dark eyes rested on her. "The day needs to come when you walk in that back door and tell *me* what to do first."

"You've been here so long that nobody needs to walk in and tell you what to do first," Jillian said. But she understood what Lenora was saying. She tried to not let it terrify her, even though it really did. Checking the counter to make sure it was free of flour, she leaned against it. "Do you honestly think I can get there, Lenora?"

The older woman walked over to check the dough in the mixers. "What you think matters more than what I think, and you need to get that settled in your mind. Is being a baker and small-business owner what you truly want?"

Why did Jillian always seem to ask what she thought was a simple question and get an entire world to consider in Lenora's answer? She poked some renegade hair back under the net. "I like not being in a corporate setting anymore, and I like some of the creative aspects of being here." She eyed the giant ovens. "Other parts scare me, and I wonder if I'll ever get to the point where it feels natural and effortless, like it does with you."

Lenora chuckled as she switched off the mixers and lifted the hooks clear. "If you decide to put as many years into this business as I have, you can do it, or I wouldn't be wasting my time trying to teach your skinny little self. I value my sanity more than that."

Relief at the baker's words flowed through her. "That helps. Thanks." Jillian looked around the now-familiar kitchen. "But for today, can you tell me where to start, knowing I'll get bossy soon enough?"

"There are some pumpkin spice doughnuts that need dipping." Lenora shook her head. "People act like the world would disintegrate if October wasn't full of pumpkin. Pumpkin muffins, pumpkin doughnuts, pumpkin coffee, pumpkin soap for their kitchens, pumpkin air fresheners for their cars."

"So don't forget to make the pumpkin bread," Jillian added and darted away to the steel workstation as the end of a towel snapped her way. She went to the dipping station with a smile on her lips, while Lenora went back to the bread. Just as Jillian was getting into a good rhythm of dipping, she heard a loud rumble outside. "I thought the air felt different out there," she said.

"Didn't you check the forecast on that fancy phone of yours this morning?" said Lenora. "Big storm blowing in from the Atlantic." They heard another rumble, then a closer, louder boom.

Jillian's hands paused. "I'd say it has arrived."

"It'll blow over soon enough. So get back to dippin.'"

She picked up another pumpkin doughnut, dipped it in the cinnamon maple frosting, and set it on the tray. "This is actually kind of cozy, like—"

There was a brilliant flash, followed almost simultaneously by a crack so loud that Jillian could feel the building shake under her feet. The power went out, leaving them in the predawn darkness. "Uh, Lenora, where are you?" She lowered the doughnut in her hand, feeling for the tray with the other. Taking the plastic gloves from her hands, she dug her phone out of her pocket and turned it on for light.

"Here, take this. It'll work better than that little thing." Jillian could barely see Lenora's hand in the darkness, but she felt the solid weight of a heavy flashlight against her arm and grasped it.

"Thanks. Did the building just get hit by lightning?"

"Or the transformer." The area in front of Lenora was suddenly illuminated by the light in her hand. "I'm going to go check."

Another pulsing flash of lightning was almost instantly followed by angry-sounding thunder.

"Are you sure? Why don't you let it settle down first?" She set the flashlight on its wide base so it stood upright like a small lamp. It wasn't bright enough for the finer detail work of cake decorating, but Jillian thought it would be fine for doughnut dipping. She tried one and was satisfied with the results, so she kept working.

Lenora started toward the back door. "It sounded different, and I want to see what the damage is." Sheets of rain blew against the windows. She pushed the door open, but the wind caught the door and jerked it out of her hands, blowing it against the outside wall with a resounding thud.

Jillian jumped, almost dropping the doughnut she was holding into the frosting. She hopped from her stool and ran over to help Lenora tug the door shut. She couldn't keep herself from ducking when lightning lit up their surroundings again. "Did you see anything in the flash?"

Lenora leaned against the wall. "No, I guess I'll have to wait." She looked in the general direction of the mixers. "I sure hope this doesn't last long or we'll have a lot of catching up to do."

To Jillian, it felt like the storm raged for hours, but according to her phone, it wasn't actually that long before it moved away. The sun was just rising when they first poked their heads outside and then ventured out into the alleyway. The first thing Jillian noticed was the tall pine tree that stood at the back of the bakery and the hardware store. A long vertical gash ran down its trunk, and a scorched patch scarred the edges.

"Well, that tree was hit," Jillian said, stating the painfully obvious.

"It wasn't the only thing," Lenora yelled over to her from across the parking lot. She pointed to a line of holes in the parking lot where chunks of pavement had been blown out by some powerful force. "I think it hit the tree and jumped over to the water line. Into the shops too, probably." She rubbed her face, staring at the damage.

"I'll call the power company." Jillian had never seen anything quite like that before. When she noticed how far some of the chunks of asphalt had been blown, she ran over to her Prius and Lenora's car, and was relieved to see only a few small pebble-sized pieces had landed on them, doing little damage. She carefully picked them off before returning to the bakery. As far as she could tell, most of the stores were completely dark, except for battery-run emergency exit signs.

After waiting in the queue to talk to someone at the utilities emergency number, she shared what little information she had been told. "The automated information assistant says not to expect the electricity to be restored until Monday and maybe not even then, depending on the damage."

"If you can believe something that's more robot than human," Lenora said. "Well, it sounds like I'll be visiting my grandbaby for the weekend." Living in the apartment above the bakery hadn't turned out to be so convenient this time. "We'll just put away what we can. Not much else we can do." She sighed and went to wash her hands.

"I'll take care of it," Jillian said. "Go call your son and pack what you need."

Lenora sighed and took the netting off her head. "Sometimes the Lord does shake things up. I wonder what He's up to now."

Later, Jillian called Bertie and told her what had happened at the shop. She and Cornelia arrived soon afterward with several coolers to load the perishable items. Jillian always wondered why two older ladies needed more than one refrigerator. Now she understood. She knew she should be more concerned with the loss of sales, especially since they'd just begun the renovations. But she was even more frustrated at the realization that the Sweetie Pies would not be able to meet on Sunday with no electricity.

Once they found a place for everything in the appliances back at Belle Haven, Jillian sat in the breakfast nook, drinking coffee.

Cornelia sat down beside her. "Don't worry. We'll bounce back from this. Bertie's seen much worse over the years."

Jillian nodded. "I know it'll all work out somehow. As strange as it might sound, I'm sorry about having to cancel the meeting tomorrow."

"Cancel?" Cornelia laughed. "It takes more than a lightning strike to keep the Sweetie Pies down and out. Bertie's already on it, calling the members to find an alternative place to meet." She patted Jillian's arm. "Don't worry, you'll have your baking lesson tomorrow." She gave Jillian one last smile of encouragement and left the room.

Jillian was deep in thought about her earlier conversation with Lenora when the front bell rang. Who would be coming here on a messy Saturday morning? Glancing at the time, she saw it was nine o'clock and remembered Cornelia telling her that Albert wanted to work today.

She hurried to the door. "Hi, Albert. You're dedicated, coming out in this crazy weather." Although the violent lightning had passed to the west, the wind and rain were still causing problems.

"Doesn't matter what kind of weather it is for indoor work, as long as we have power." Albert took off an orange rain slicker and shook the water off it, stomping mud from his work boots before stepping inside. "Working on a beauty like Belle Haven beats getting under my sister's feet while she cleans."

Jillian took the slicker and hung it on the clothes tree next to the door. Belle Haven had more rooms than a hunting dog had fleas, but closets weren't in style during the antebellum period. "Josi has the day off?"

"She goes in at noon," Albert said, his tool kit hanging at his side. "She blows through the house like a cleaning tornado before she leaves. Makes a fellow feel lazy."

Jillian walked with him to the room he was repurposing for their office. It looked a mess, but she knew it was just a part of the process. "This will keep you too busy for laziness. Holler if you need anything." After his experience with Bertie the day before, she figured the best thing she could do was run interference with Bertie and give the man some space. She could get a look at his work after he'd had some time to work free from distraction.

She had spent a good portion of the day reading the history books Josi had found for her when Bertie came to tell her Annalise Reed had offered her kitchen for the Sweetie Pies meeting at the regular time. "Josi's making the treat, but we'll also spend some time sharing the tips and basics that helped us become skilled bakers."

Jillian realized she'd never been to a Sweetie Pies meeting that involved actual baking or instruction. They mostly shared a dessert together and socialized. The women were changing their agenda for her sake. Leaning over, she kissed her grandmother lightly on her soft cheek, smelling rosewater. "Thank you, Bertie."

Her grandmother looked surprised. "Nothing to it. A few

calls is all it took." She left the room, heading for the new office. Jillian decided to let Bertie have one chance at nosing around before she intervened.

By the time the Belle Haven women left for the funeral home, the fearsome wind had gone, leaving only a light rain. *The sky may be the only one crying on the night of Otis Dupree's visitation*, Jillian thought as Bertie drove through the puddles.

Wearing a black dress with Peter Pan collar and fussy sleeves, Cornelia reached out to finger the material of Jillian's new dress. "This black one is lovely, dear. Much more respectful than that navy number you wore to the funeral home the last time. But it's a little long, though, don't you think?"

Jillian had been caught off guard almost immediately after arriving back in Moss Hollow. That was when Nadine Belmont Wilson, an old high school adversary, had died. Jillian had had only one black dress in her wardrobe, and it was more suited to a romantic night on the town than a funeral. She had worn a navy-blue outfit instead of the traditional black. It was a good thing she'd gone shopping shortly after that bleak affair, as here she was, needing it a few short months later.

"One inch below the knees hardly qualifies as long," Jillian said. Her great-aunt apparently wanted her to dress both respectfully and enticingly in case any eligible men happened to be hanging out at the mortuary—like Hunter Greyson. "I refuse to use a solemn occasion like a visitation to try to attract a man."

Cornelia opened her mouth, but before she could say a word, Bertie beat a fist on the steering wheel and snapped, "That is enough!"

"We're sorry, Bertie," Cornelia said meekly. "You're right." She primly folded her gloved hands in her lap and stared out the window, silent for the rest of the ride.

There was no receiving line at the funeral home since Otis was the last of his family. The only person at the casket was a representative of Greyson & Sons.

Jillian wondered what had happened to Frederick's family. She'd never considered if Frederick's wife, Charlotte, had stayed in Moss Hollow with her child, never to know what had happened to her husband. Perhaps she had thought he'd left secretly in the night to avoid family conflict, traveled north and joined the Union forces. If so, she might surmise, when he didn't return from the war, that he had been killed in one of the horrific battles. How had Jedediah been able to look her in the face, knowing he was the cause of her pain and confusion?

The thought of such a long family line that had contributed so much to the development of Moss Hollow and the surrounding area vanishing from the earth forever chilled Jillian.

There was a light touch on her arm. Jillian looked up into Savannah's concerned brown eyes. "How are you doing, Jillian? I heard the shop was struck by lightning while you were inside! That would have freaked me out."

"Well, that's not exactly true," Jillian explained. "The lightning hit the pine behind the bakery and the hardware store. Lenora thinks the electricity traveled along the tree and then jumped to the water line and into the buildings, knocking out the power. I just hope it's something the utility company will fix quickly and that nothing in the bakery was damaged so we're not out a fortune. Of course this had to happen now that we've started renovations on Belle Haven."

The empathetic look in her friend's eyes almost brought tears to her own. "Let me know if there's anything I can do."

"You can come with me to see Otis. I need to get it over with. Not that there's any family to insult by skipping it. I still feel like I should."

She and Savannah joined the viewing line for the man who had seemingly hidden any goodness inside him like a miser and had embraced the love of power instead. Reaching the coffin and gazing down at Otis, Jillian thought he looked so small, dwarfed by the elaborate bronze casket and tufted satin lining. His cane was tucked beside him, and the knowledge of its wicked hidden blade made Jillian shudder. But it was fitting that the weapon, which in the end had not kept him safe, was to be buried with him.

Jillian and Savannah made their way to the refreshment table. Jillian's throat was tightening, and she needed something to drink. As she poured a cup of coffee, the sound of a commotion reached them from across the room. Savannah glanced over, and a look of disgust came over her face. "Ted the Ferret has the nerve to come here, and he's been drinking to boot. Nothing he does should surprise me."

"Maybe he came to gloat," Jillian whispered to her. "We need to listen to every sodden word he says. Maybe his loose lips will give something away."

The two women wove through the crowd, positioning themselves to watch and listen closely.

The councilman first bowed clumsily to the attendant. Then he edged toward the coffin. "You thought you got away with it, didn't you, old man? You didn't even have time to throw it in my face before you got what was coming to you."

Jillian exchanged a look with Savannah, and the people around them whispered. The attendant raised one hand, obviously a signal to Hunter, who was standing in a side room in the wings. Hunter moved quickly toward the front of the line.

Ted turned toward Hunter as the mortician placed a firm hand upon his shoulder. "He bribed her. I know he did," Ted said.

Jillian wasn't sure if he was speaking to Hunter or just throwing his words into the air. Ted turned back to Otis, straining against the arms of the men who were pulling him away from the scene.

"Well, now you're dead and gone, you old goat!" He swiped a hand across his mouth. "And I'm glad you're dead. There's nothing you can do to stop me now."

Before Ted was pulled from the room, his attention turned toward a slight woman who looked to be in her thirties. "You Jezebel!" He spit out the words. "You think being Otis Dupree's lackey is the way to succeed? You'll regret sabotaging my loan. Just you wait. Kiss your job good-bye and forget about finding another one in this town!"

He might have gone on haranguing the horrified woman, but Hunter tightened his grip, one that Jillian knew was more forceful than his calm face indicated. "Come with me, Councilman."

As soon as the yammering ferret man was escorted from the room, people crowded around the woman. "What did Ted mean, Shelly?" Jillian overheard one woman ask. *Shelly*, Jillian thought. *Dorothy had said Otis had referenced a bank employee by that name.* She must be the link between Otis and Ted.

Eyes glazed, Shelly looked over those crowding against her. She burst into tears and ran from the room.

"I'm going after her," Jillian whispered to Savannah, following the distraught woman. "Shelly, wait!" She raised her voice but kept it as calm as possible.

The woman pushed open the outer door and stumbled into the memorial garden, still sobbing.

Jillian grabbed a box of tissues from the last pew at the back of the hall before dashing out after her. She glanced around at the winding paths and gentle fountains, looking for the distraught woman. Movement on the far side of the garden alerted her to Shelly's position, and she slowed down to approach gently. Shelly sat on a stone bench, her head in her hands.

Jillian lowered to sit beside her. "I have some tissues." She held out the box.

"Thank you." Shelly sniffled, then reached out a small hand to pull some tissues from the box. She blew her nose several times. Jillian sat quietly, giving her time to compose herself.

The woman dabbed at the corner of an eye and glanced over at Jillian. "I don't know you, do I?"

"I'm Jillian Green, Bertie Harper's granddaughter. You probably know her."

Her shoulders relaxed noticeably. "Oh, Mrs. Harper. My son loves the doughnuts at her shop."

Jillian smiled. "I've eaten my fair share of them myself."

The two women fell silent for a few minutes, Jillian trying not to spook the woman.

"I didn't do what Ted said," Shelly said quietly after a while.

"So he just assumed you sabotaged his loan since you work at the bank?"

Shelly dabbed at her eyes again with a corner of the tissue. "I'm a loan officer, so it's not like people haven't been mad at me before when their loans are rejected. That's because they don't understand the loan process. But you'd think someone in politics would understand the banking business better." She drew in a shuddering breath. "Unfortunately, he has just enough truth to do more damage than I can afford in this small town."

"What do you mean?" Jillian asked gently.

Words began to pour from the woman faster than the water from the serenity fountains. "Otis approached me and offered me a bribe to make sure Ted's loan didn't go through."

"How much did he offer you?"

The woman stared out at the garden, which was bathed in soft lights for the early evening. Jillian wondered if she should have kept the question for later. But Shelly answered.

"It wasn't an exact amount. You see, my ten-year-old son was diagnosed with leukemia a couple of months ago."

"I'm so sorry," Jillian whispered.

Shelly nodded and continued. "His father left three years ago, so it's just us. Otis found out and offered to pay all of Jonah's medical bills if I wouldn't authorize the loan."

"And you didn't take him up on his offer," Jillian said.

"No, I didn't. I couldn't." Shelly's face begged her to believe what she said. "I told Otis having a good, steady job was worth more to me than any promises he could make. He was angry, but I didn't give in."

"So Otis got what he wanted for free?"

Shelly shrugged. "I honestly don't know why he even felt that a bribe was needed." She paused to wipe her nose again. "Maybe he didn't know how hard it is for most people to get a loan, given his wealth. But even being a successful businessman or a politician doesn't mean it's a sure thing. There's a whole committee that has to agree to approve a loan. It's much worse to agree to a potentially bad loan than to reject one that might turn out okay."

"That's what they call risk management, right?" Jillian asked.

The woman nodded. "It's part of it."

"So if your actions were all lawful and according to your employer's guidelines, why were you so upset at the councilman's accusations, as unpleasant as they were?"

"You know how it is in a small town," Shelly said. "My son goes to school with the children of people who heard what Ted said. Even if they see I'm not arrested or fired from my job, they'll still talk about me, and then their children will take the stories to school." Her eyes misted again. "Jonah has enough to deal with, what with the disease and the chemo and everything. He doesn't need kids asking him if his mother is a crook."

"Shelly, do you think Ted is capable of physically hurting someone, maybe even killing them?"

The woman's eyes hardened. "I wouldn't put anything past Ted Grady. And if he comes near my home or threatens me, I'll get a restraining order so fast, it'll make his head spin!" She peered at her watch. "I need to go now. I told the sitter I'd be home soon. Thank you for your kindness."

"You're welcome. I know what it's like to be misunderstood."

"I hope I see you around town."

"Bring Jonah to the bakery sometime and he can pick out a treat."

"I will." The women stood and walked back toward the main building, then Shelly veered right to head toward the parking lot. Jillian watched Shelly leave, a petite woman carrying so much on her narrow shoulders. The old adage was true. No matter how hard things got, there was always someone who was in worse straits.

She turned to enter the viewing room but stopped when she heard Hunter call her name. He was waving to her from the doorway of his office. "Jillian, we need you here."

Jillian hurried down the hall. What had Cornelia done now?

When she entered, Bertie was the focus of everyone's attention. She lay stretched out on the dark leather sofa, a cloth covering her eyes. "Bertie! Are you okay?" Jillian rushed to her grandmother.

"I'm fine. Everyone's overreacting." Her spit and fire were still intact, but she sounded tired.

Cornelia was perched on the arm of the sofa near Bertie's head. "People who are *fine* don't faint and almost tumble into a casket! Have you had your blood pressure checked in the last six months?" She grabbed her sister's wrist and pressed two fingers against it. "You were whiter than Otis before you fell, and you're none too rosy even now."

Bertie snatched her wrist from Cornelia's grasp. "That's because I have the complexion of a fine Southern gentlewoman," she grated out between tight lips. "You know I don't over-tan my skin in the sun like someone else I know."

Hunter drew Jillian aside. "I did check Bertie's blood pressure," he said. "While it was a little elevated, it wasn't high enough to worry about. But she did faint, so keep an eye on her. It might also be a good idea to get her blood-sugar levels checked."

Jillian thanked him for his help. "I'll encourage her to see her doctor, but my grandmother does what she does. Old dogs, new tricks, and all of that, you know."

Hunter smiled, his blue eyes warm with understanding and a spark of humor. "Imagine that." He looked around her to address the twin sisters. "I think Bertie can go home safely, although someone else should drive, just to be safe."

"I will," said Jillian. "Bertie, why don't you try to sit up for a minute while I go tell Savannah we're leaving, and then we'll walk you to the car."

Her grandmother huffed. "I know how to walk. I don't need to be coddled." She pushed herself to a sitting position, swaying. "But I'll wait for you here while you talk to Savannah." When Jillian didn't leave immediately, she waved a hand at her. "Go on now."

Jillian found Savannah sitting with Harold Johnson, talking quietly.

"How's Bertie?" Savannah asked immediately.

"Still a little shaky, but she should be all right. I hope she'll get a checkup if this sort of thing happens again. I just came to tell you we're leaving."

Savannah nodded. "I'm glad she's okay. I've never seen Bertie like that before. It scared me." Glancing toward Harold, she added, "I'll see you tomorrow."

Jillian understood it to mean, "We'll talk tomorrow."

"Good." She turned to Harold. "I'll see you around, Harold."

"Take care, Jillian," the outdoorsman said, looking like he couldn't wait to shed his somber suit and sit on the porch for a while. *Come to think of it*, Jillian thought, *I'd like to do exactly the same thing.*

By breakfast the next morning, Bertie was her old self again, grumbling whenever Jillian or Cornelia looked at her for longer than a nanosecond.

"I was only checking to see if you needed syrup for your pancakes," Jillian said defensively. "I can tell you're fully recovered." She held up her hand when her grandmother started to speak. "After this, I'll say no more about it. But please make sure you are taking care of yourself as much as you take care of everyone else."

Bertie's eyes softened, and she nodded. "I will make more of an effort. Now, make sure you're ready for church on time."

That was the best Jillian could have hoped for. From that moment on, it was as though the excitement of the night before had never happened, and the day of rest was truly restful for Jillian. So when the Sweetie Pies gathered at Annalise's gracious home a few blocks from the center of Moss Hollow, she was eager to learn from the others.

Annalise met them at the cheerful red door of her two story brick home. A small plaque to the left of the door read *1872*.

"Come on in. Lenora and Josi are already here." As they walked through the center hall, Jillian stopped for a look at the main staircase of the historic home. It was much narrower and less ornate than the one at Belle Haven, but the gleaming wood banister traced such an interesting line that Jillian was compelled to pause for a longer look while her grandmother and great-aunt continued into the kitchen.

"Is this the staircase Albert restored, Annalise?" she asked their hostess.

"Yes, and didn't he do it splendidly?" Annalise answered. "Bertie and Cornelia saw it before, but you haven't. If you'd like, I can show you some photos."

"I'd love to see them."

Annalise pulled her phone from the floral apron she was wearing and launched her photo gallery. Flipping to the first picture, she gave the phone to Jillian.

"Wow, I see what you mean," Jillian said as she scrolled through the transformation of the charming staircase. "It's like Cinderella. The bone structure of beauty was already there. Albert just cleaned off the ashes and dressed it in a gorgeous ball gown."

Annalise chuckled. "That's a fanciful way of putting it. I'll have to remember that."

Jillian gave Annalise her phone back, and they walked into the kitchen. "Hi, Lenora. How's your visit with your son going?"

The tall woman leaned against the marble island. "It's noisy and chaotic, and I'm loving every moment . . . as long as it doesn't last too long."

"Josi, this cake is gorgeous," Cornelia said as they gathered to admire the tall, double-layer cake, iced to perfection. "It's too pretty to cut."

"I hope you haven't had red velvet cake too recently," the librarian said. "It's a favorite of Albert's and mine."

Annalise set a silver coffeepot on the island, next to a collection of cups and saucers. "Has Albert mentioned how the Belle Haven renovation is going, Josi?"

The quiet woman's eyes lit up. "Oh, he's in his element. He fell asleep over dinner tonight because he was up so late going over his work plans. It's what he loves to do." She lifted the glass covering off the cake and turned to Jillian. "Thank you for accepting his bid, even though we're so new to town."

"We enjoyed seeing his enthusiasm for the project we decided to start with," Cornelia said, looking eagerly at the rich red cake and cream cheese frosting. "And I think Albert will be able to hear what the house tells him to do." She glanced over at her sister. "Not everyone has the ear, you know."

Josi handed a plate to Cornelia, her eyes a little puzzled. "Thank you. I'm looking forward to all the progress photos, just like the ones Annalise took."

Jillian turned to Josi, an idea growing. "Has Albert considered putting examples of his work on a website, for marketing? Before and after photos are gold for businesses like his. I found plenty of positive reviews of Albert's work, but having those visuals right on his own website would bring him a lot of business."

"He should listen to Jillian," Savannah said. "When it comes to marketing, she really knows how to sell the sizzle."

A knock at the front door sent Annalise scurrying out of the room. She returned a moment later with Laura Lee.

"How are you, dear?" Cornelia greeted the deputy. "You're looking a little peaked."

The younger woman gave a weary smile. "Storms sometimes blow in trouble, and we've been working nonstop this weekend all over the county."

"Why aren't you at home getting some rest?" Jillian asked.

Laura Lee climbed onto one of the swivel stools at the island. "Because there comes a point where having a little fun is more important than rest."

"I think someone needs to point that out to Gooder," Savannah said, surprising Jillian. "I think he needs to take more time to relax. Stress can be deadly."

Annalise waved her fork toward them. "You two are so right. I've been trying to get that across to Byron for years. He's been healthy so far, but I'm afraid it'll catch up to him if he's not willing to make some changes."

Jillian concentrated on keeping her gaze far away from her grandmother.

"Why don't you refuse to cook Byron's meals until he goes to yoga classes with you?" Laura Lee asked, evoking laughter all around.

Annalise laughed along. "Hmmm, would a pair of yoga pants fit in Byron's Christmas stocking, do you think?"

"The one who really needs some rest and relaxation is Shelly from the bank," said Savannah.

Annalise looked up from pouring some coffee for Laura Lee. "Do you mean Shelly DeLeon, the loan officer?"

Savannah nodded. "Ted Grady acted horribly toward her last night at Otis Dupree's visitation. That on top of caring for a sick son alone and all. Her stress level must be through the roof."

"I heard that Ted was on a tear last night," said Annalise, "but not that Shelly was his target. That's simply reprehensible."

"Well, Otis first and then Shelly. He accused her of sabotaging his loan application so that it was rejected," Jillian said.

Annalise shook her head. "That's impossible. One person doesn't have that kind of power. That's why the loan applications are reviewed and voted on by a committee. It protects the bank, as well as the patrons. What in the world could Ted be trying to accomplish by attacking her character like that? Poor Shelly; she works so hard. Byron's said he wishes he could find fifty more like her." She picked up the serrated knife and cut herself another, smaller piece of cake.

"I can't give any details, but it's obvious Grady's been slipping downhill for a while," Laura Lee said between bites. "With his behavior last night, I give him zero chance of reelection when his term is up."

Lenora nodded her agreement. "My cousin Jasmine told me Ted called her one night and asked if she could meet him for an emergency hair appointment. Offered her double her usual charge. When she got to the salon, half his hair was hacked off like he'd tried to do it with a machete. And he smelled awful, like alcohol and gasoline."

"What in God's good green earth had he been up to?" asked Bertie.

"Jasmine said he was harder to follow than a wild turkey on a moonless night, but it seems that our councilman had tried filling his gas tank after imbibing too much and fell asleep at the pump. He woke up when a stream of gasoline hit him on the side of the head. When he couldn't get the smell out, he tried to cut out the smelly bits." She shook her head. "It's only a matter of time before that man does some serious damage."

Jillian wondered if he already had.

"I thought Jasmine had gone a little heavy on the potpourri last time I was in for my appointment," said Cornelia. "Now that I know why, it's impressive she got that much of the gas smell cleared."

"Don't those pumps have automatic shutoffs?" Jillian asked. "I usually clean out my Prius while I fill up."

Laura Lee shook a finger at her. "Resist that temptation, Jillian. The shutoffs usually work, but they do malfunction sometimes. Just like Ted discovered. The risk isn't worth it, in my opinion."

"After Lenora's story, I think I'll change my ways," Jillian assured them.

Savannah set her empty plate on the white marble. "So, are we going to give Jillian the tips you asked us to bring, Annalise?"

Jillian looked around. "What do you mean?"

"Oh, heavens, I forgot." Annalise started pulling items from her cabinet—bowls, measuring cups and spoons, baking ingredients—and putting them to one side of the island. "I asked everyone to bring a baking tip for you to use while we talk you through a simple spice cake recipe. Reviewing the basics of baking is like opera singers running through their scales every day." She whirled over to the stainless steel refrigerator and took out some eggs.

"Well, we should start with mine, then," said Laura Lee. She handed an index card to Jillian.

"'Don't use cold eggs,'" Jillian read. "'Place them in a bowl of warm water for ten to fifteen minutes.'"

The ladies nodded their approval. Jillian filled one of the small bowls Annalise had provided with warm water. "How many eggs do we need?"

"Two," Annalise said, and Jillian carefully placed them in the water. While the eggs warmed, the women shared other tips: how best to butter pans; the importance of spooning flour into a measuring cup rather than dipping the cup into the flour container; rotating cake pans during baking, but not until after two-thirds of the baking time had passed to be sure the cake is set; cooling cakes upside down to flatten for even layers.

When the eggs were ready, Jillian referred to the tip cards as she followed the recipe Annalise had given her, joking with the other Sweetie Pies as she worked and they encouraged. It reminded her of one of those reality cooking shows where the audience shouts advice while cooks battle to make the winning dish. Except in this case, the entire audience was on her side.

She was hand-beating the moist batter and listening to a lively discussion on the use of vanilla extract versus powdered vanilla bean when she splattered some batter onto her blouse. "Oh no. This is one of my favorite blouses."

Annalise handed her a clean dishcloth. "The powder room is down the hall on the left."

Jillian dashed to the small room and dampened the cloth Annalise had given her, hoping the batter wouldn't leave a stain. She scraped the excess off with a fingernail and then dabbed the fabric carefully with the cloth. *Jillian, you really need to learn to listen without getting wrapped up in the conversation.*

Waiting for the spots to air-dry a little to see how the stain was reacting to her efforts, Jillian looked around the small but pleasant room with one wall of exposed brick sporting framed pieces of ink drawings and calligraphy.

Her heart jumped when she realized one of the framed pieces held a meticulously rendered copy of the same quote from *Henry IV* that had been stitched as a wall hanging at the Dupree mansion. Setting the cloth down, she leaned in for a closer look at the piece, carefully lifting it from the wall to examine the back. It was signed *Mary Louise Stansel 1861*. Where had Annalise come across it?

After returning the calligraphy to its place, Jillian finished doctoring her blouse as quickly as she could and returned to the kitchen. She paid close attention to the task at hand and soon slid the pan into the oven and set the timer. As the ladies chatted amongst themselves, she pulled Annalise aside. "While I was waiting for my blouse to dry, I enjoyed reading all the calligraphies on the wall of your powder room. I might talk to Bertie and Cornelia about doing something similar in the new office. The quote from Shakespeare was an interesting choice, and it looked like an antique. Where did you find it?"

Annalise's face brightened. "Thank you for the compliment. It took me a while to collect the different pieces. Except the one you mentioned, actually. That one is a family heirloom and was done by one of my ancestors, Mary Stansel."

"I know women from prosperous families at that time were often encouraged to study the classics and art," said Jillian, thinking of Bridgett's journal comments about being a cultured young woman. "Do you know why your ancestor chose that particular line of Shakespeare?"

Annalise nodded. "I do, actually. A few years ago, I read an article about minimalism and got the idea to go through everything in my house and keep only the things that I really loved or needed." She looked around at her spacious living area. "When your family has lived in the same house for almost 150 years, you're going to find stuff you never knew existed. I found an old hat box of letters, all written to Mary from people all over Georgia." She lowered her voice. "They all talked about her contribution to the Union cause. A hummingbird could have knocked me over. Several of them had the same quote written under the writer's signature. So I did a little research and learned Union sympathizers used that as a way of identifying themselves."

The contrast in reactions amazed Jillian. Otis had ordered Dorothy to destroy the words stitched in navy thread. Annalise had displayed those same words in a room built for the use of visitors. "What did you think when you first learned about it?" she asked.

"Initially, I was horrified. Me, married to a man whose family contributed to the town statue dedicated to the Sons of the South?" Annalise gave a low whistle. "Well, considering your own family line, I'm sure you can imagine."

"I certainly can."

"But then I thought about how complicated human beings are and how important it is to learn the lessons of the past. So when I found the calligraphy signed by Mary in another room, I knew I wanted to display it where people could see it and ask about it. Maybe then they would think about its truth, even if only for a minute or two, while they checked for spinach between their teeth."

Jillian had never realized Annalise was such a deep thinker. She'd mistaken her love of bright colors and chronic cheerfulness as signs of a person who lived a rather superficial life.

"I have been doing some research that led me to talk with

Otis Dupree about one of his ancestors," Jillian said. "In fact, I had returned to the Dupree estate for a second time for that reason when I discovered Otis's body."

"How terrible!"

"Then, a few days ago, I went back to talk to his housekeeper, Dorothy, and she showed me an embroidered work with exactly the same quote and an inscription on the back, *For Frederick, 1861.* Frederick Dupree was also a Union sympathizer who died at the hands of his own brother, Jedediah, as Frederick was heading north to join the Union forces."

"I've lived here my whole life, and I've never heard that before."

"I only know about it because it was recounted in the diary of Bridgett Summerlin, a niece of the Belles who lived in Belle Haven during that time. Bridgett and Jedediah were apparently an 'item' at the time. Long story short, I now think someone in the Dupree family stitched the wall hanging as a way of memorializing Frederick. Perhaps his wife, Charlotte. I related all of this to Otis, and he apparently went ballistic. He ransacked the mansion until he found it and then ordered Dorothy to destroy it."

"Destroy something tied to your family for over 150 years? It sounds like Otis was not only meaner than a boxed-in bear. He may have been downright crazy."

"I know. Dorothy thought better of it and held onto it, just for the sake of history. I have photos of it on my camera if you'd like to see."

"Oh, that would be great!" Annalise exclaimed.

Just then the timer for the oven began beeping. "I guess we're going to have to get back to the kitchen," Jillian said. "You've really helped me, Annalise. I'm going to keep digging until I find how my family and the Duprees were connected to this little mystery. And while I'm at it, maybe I'll poke around Belle Haven and see if I can find a wall's worth of interesting things to display as well."

Jillian hurried to the oven and carefully removed the pans, realizing she'd been too preoccupied to rotate them. But as she placed the layers on a cooling rack—upside down as one of her tips from the Sweetie Pies advised—she was relieved to see they had still cooked evenly. They weren't even the slightest bit burnt. The rest of the club members gathered around to congratulate her on her success.

"We know you can make a fine frosting," Laura Lee said, "so I'd say our first class has been a huge success."

Jillian had to agreed, although not for same reason.

Cornelia burst into the kitchen Monday morning, Possum clasped to her bosom. Bertie, who was on the phone with the utility company, placed a hand over the mouthpiece and hissed "Shhh!" at her.

Jillian threw her great-aunt an apologetic look from where she sat, eating a bowl of cereal. They needed to know whether the shop's utilities would be in working order so they could prepare for business, but her grandmother could have been gentler about it.

"If it is necessary, we will make do," Bertie said. "No, there is nothing else you can help me with." She replaced the handset of the kitchen phone and groaned. "Another day down the drain. They say we will have power for sure tomorrow. I only hope they're right."

"I'm sorry, Bertie," Cornelia said, sitting at the breakfast table, still holding on to the chubby cat. "But I have some good news to balance out the not so good." She massaged under Possum's chin, watching the cat stretch his head forward with eyes closed in feline bliss.

Bertie slumped into a chair across from her twin and propped her chin in her hand. "What is it, Sister?"

"Raymond and I had a chat this morning, and he told me to restore Belle Haven to its former glory. Isn't that wonderful?" She beamed down at the cat and then over at her sister.

"Did Uncle Raymond happen to mention where he buried the gold to pay for it?" Jillian asked, trying to lighten Bertie's mood and bring Cornelia back to reality.

"Wouldn't that be wonderful if he did, that rascal? But you don't need money when you have enough friends."

"That's a nice sentiment," Jillian said, not sure what else to say. "But buried gold might be quicker." She carried her empty bowl to the sink. "I need to run an errand in town, but I won't be gone long."

Bertie nodded gloomily. "Run all the errands you want. You have all day now." She heaved her diminutive body out of the seat, as though it had turned to stone. "I need to call Lenora and let her know she should stay at her son's another day." She made the call in her usual efficient way before padding out of the kitchen.

Cornelia lowered Possum to the floor, and he trotted over to his water dish, lapping up the drink with a bright-pink tongue. "She'll snap out of it as soon as Albert arrives and she has someone to supervise again." Cornelia crossed over to the refrigerator and pulled out a leftover slice of quiche lorraine. "I'll be spending most of the day in the gardens. With all the rain we had, the weeds will be growing like crazy, and I can't let them get a foothold."

"They won't know what hit 'em." Jillian thought of the delicious wilted dandelion greens she'd had at Harold's gator feast. "Maybe I'll come help you when I'm back from town." Maybe she'd keep the nutritious weeds to eat with her lunch this time, instead of tossing them in with the other garden debris.

Cornelia smiled at her over the plate of quiche. "That would be nice, dear."

Jillian drove to town with thoughts about the shop, Belle Haven's future, Bridgett, Frederick, and Otis all jumbling together. She still didn't know where Frederick was buried at Belle Haven, and with Otis dead too, what would they do with the remains, even if they found the grave? But it still felt wrong for Frederick's resting place to be unmarked, as though his life had never mattered. His brother was probably entombed in the massive Dupree crypt right in the center of the town's cemetery. Shouldn't Frederick be there as well?

At Greyson & Sons Funeral Home, Jillian once again walked along the empty halls. "What a pleasant surprise." Turning, Jillian saw Hunter had entered the hall from one of the smaller viewing rooms. "How's Bertie doing today?"

"Back to her old self. She promised she would try to be better at taking care of herself, but I'll believe it when I see it."

Hunter opened his office door, holding it for Jillian to enter before him. "I hope she'll follow through on that." He waited for Jillian to take a seat before taking his own behind the large desk. "So, to what do I owe this pleasure? Have you made progress in your research about the journal?"

"Some, but I still have a long way to go. You might say that my attention was pulled away at the visitation for Otis Dupree."

Hunter quirked an eyebrow. "Is everything okay?" When she gave a short version of what had happened outside the mortuary with Shelly while her grandmother was fainting, he smiled. "I'm glad you were there for Shelly. Ted Grady sure put her through the wringer, as if she hadn't been through enough already." He paused before continuing. "Now, tell me about your research."

She showed him the photos of the framed Shakespeare quote she had taken at the Dupree estate and told him about her discovery at the Reeds' home and the story of Annalise's family.

Hunter listened intently, and his smile grew. "That's excellent. You know who Mary Stansel is from Bridgett's journal and even know one of her descendents. Historians can work for years and not make such progress."

Jillian gave a rueful chuckle. "But it only makes me want to know more."

"Ah, be careful." The handsome mortician wagged a finger at her. "You're on the edge of becoming a history junkie. It's a very slippery slope."

"Once I find out what happened to Bridgett, and if she did become a secret Yankee while she was in Moss Hollow, I'll stop. I promise."

Hunter shook his head. "That's what we all say, Jillian. 'I can stop anytime.'"

Jillian thought being a self-proclaimed history junkie looked pretty good on the man sitting before her, so she wasn't terribly motivated to worry about it. "I still haven't found anything displaying the *Henry IV* quote at Belle Haven." She told him about her sneaky tour of the second-floor rooms, trying to discover which one had been Bridgett's. "I'm not sure where to look next."

"You know, there is the real possibility that she never converted to the Union cause. She was, after all, pretty serious about a young man who was a dyed-in-the-wool Confederate."

"That's true. But maybe Jedediah's violence so disappointed her that she flipped to the other side. If she did, she probably had something to indicate her secret allegiance. But where is it today?"

He was quiet for a moment, then brightened. "Whoever stitched Frederick's piece didn't put it out for everyone to see because the home was still a Confederate one. Mary displayed her piece openly because she, her husband, and her family all had Union leanings. But Bridgett was not at her own place. Displaying it boldly could have caused her trouble. Maybe she made something portable." He swiveled to a credenza behind his desk, picking up a doily from it before turning back to Jillian. "Look for something small like this. Perhaps a shawl or handkerchief. Then she could have hidden it from prying eyes."

Jillian frowned. "If that were the case, she probably took it with her when she returned to her family."

"Not necessarily," said Hunter. "After all, she left the journal her brother had made for her."

"I know, and that's bugging me too." Jillian jumped out of her seat and started pacing. "The gift from her brother was special to her. She mentions that throughout the whole journal. Yet she abandoned it." Jillian stared out the window at the memorial garden, thinking. Hunter remained quiet, letting her think. She appreciated that about him.

Then she whirled around. "What if Bridgett left the journal behind hoping someone would find it and read the truth about Frederick's disappearance?"

A slow smile spread across Hunter's face. "Now that's a reason worth leaving a treasured possession behind."

"And apparently it only took a hundred and fifty-odd years for her sacrifice to pay off. Kinda."

A light knock cut off their discussion. Hunter's assistant, Oliver Kent, entered. "Mr. and Mrs. Hall are here for their appointment."

Hunter nodded. "Thanks, Oliver. Give me a couple minutes and then send them in." When the door closed, he walked over to Jillian. "I'm sorry, but I need to go."

"Don't be." Jillian stood and started for the door. "Talking to you has given me something else to think about. Thanks."

"Let me know if I can help." Hunter opened the door for her. "I'll see you soon, I hope."

"Bye, Hunter." Jillian smiled as she left the hushed building, stepping into the morning sunshine. Since she was only a couple of blocks away from Moss Hollow Cemetery, she decided to push aside her normal aversion to cemeteries and make a quick visit to the Dupree crypt. She'd get it over with as fast as possible, like ripping a bandage from an old wound.

The Dupree crypt resembled an art museum more than a burial place, with graceful urns full of potted plants, classic columns, and a sculpture of a beautiful angel, her wings spread over the entire opening of the mausoleum. The peaceful face of the angel spoke to Jillian, and she felt stronger as she walked through the open iron gate and down the sloping entry to the main chamber of the crypt.

In the soft natural light from the open entry and a small stained glass window set into the opposite wall, she was seeing what any visitor would have seen in the late eighteen hundreds. She recognized some of the names from *The History of Moss Hollow* before finding the resting place of Jedediah Dupree, his date of death chiseled into stone: May 20, 1890, at the age of fifty-one. Jillian wondered what had taken him at a relatively young age, at least by twenty-first-century standards. Had guilt worn away his physical strength, leaving him more vulnerable to the common diseases of his day?

Jillian searched for any indication that Jedediah had had a son, but seeing none, she continued reading. She found Elliot Dupree, brother to Jedediah, whose years of life were considerably longer. Elliot must be the one through whom the family line had continued. Until Otis. Walking back into the sunshine did not wash away the sadness.

Then Jillian realized why the death of Otis Dupree had had such an effect on her. She, too, could be the last of a proud Moss Hollow family, the end of the Belle Haven family line. She turned briefly to look once again at the face of the Dupree angel, and from it she gained the strength to trust all would be as it should. She would return home and see if she could find anything else belonging to Bridgett.

Back at Belle Haven, on her way to the staircase, Jillian stopped by the new office renovation to greet Albert, who was painting the wainscoting with a foul-smelling clear liquid, his mouth and nose covered with a blue mask. When he saw her in the doorway, he paused in his work, raised his mask, and smiled. "Jillian! This will need to dry overnight, so I'll start work on the windows soon."

"That's fine, Albert. Thanks for the update. It looks like the office is going to be lovely."

He nodded, replaced the mask over his face, and resumed his work. Jillian escaped up the stairs as quickly as her legs would carry her, debating where she should begin searching again, this time in less obvious places. At some point, Jillian knew she might have to make her way to the attic again, but first, she'd try looking at the second-floor rooms from a different perspective.

She was pacing around her own room, searching every inch of the walls and furniture for anything that seemed like it could be a hiding place, when one of her steps made a different kind of squeak. *It sounds hollow!* Grabbing a metal ruler from inside her desk, Jillian used it to pry at the board. Finally, it popped up with a satisfying release. Inside was definitely a hidey hole, but it was mostly empty except for the tiny skeleton of a mouse. No family jewels, sterling silver, or personal mementos, sadly. But Jillian was glad to know it was there, though it would mean removing the current, albeit deceased, occupant. She was getting a little tired of her life revolving around bones, so she cleaned out the space and lowered the plank back in place and went to search elsewhere.

Moving on to Cornelia's room next would have been wise, while her great-aunt was out in the gardens. The longer Jillian waited, the greater the chance Cornelia would return to her room to rest. But as she walked past the room next to hers—the "psychic vibe" room as Cornelia called it—she felt its pull and slipped inside. After the find in her own bedroom, Jillian spent some time stepping and bouncing on every floorboard but heard no unusual sounds in the wooden planks. She crouched beside the metal-frame daybed, searching underneath for anything different. But other than the knowledge that far too much time had passed between dustings up here, Jillian discovered nothing.

Dropping onto the bed, Jillian stared around again. She'd already looked inside the armoire, but cocking her head to the right, she examined the exterior again. *Maybe I need to check the interior a second time,* she thought. *Bridgett was a one-time guest here. She wouldn't have known about secret hiding areas. She would use something a bit more obvious.*

She pushed the contents of the armoire to the side, once again revealing a set of cubbyholes stuffed with the accumulation of all sorts of cloth, children's toys, and the like. Then, at the back of the armoire's base she saw a pair of tiny hinges camouflaged by the bottom board and the back. Looking closely, she saw the edges of a small door in the base. She tried the metal ruler again, but the edges were much too tight. Frustrated, she slammed her fist onto the tiny door. Almost miraculously, it popped up and Jillian found a small hiding place, perhaps used in the days before there were home security systems to hide valuables or money. Running her hand into the small compartment, half afraid of finding another dead mouse, she retrieved a soft leather pouch. She sat cross-legged on the floor, clutching the prize to her chest.

Jillian's cry of triumph was cut short when Cornelia burst into the room, Possum trailing behind her. She obviously had heard odd noises from the room and had come to investigate.

"Jillian! What on earth are you doing?" With a gasp, her great-aunt snatched the pouch from Jillian's grasp. "Smart girl!

You've found Raymond's new message." Cornelia sat back on her haunches and opened the pouch. "How exciting!" She pulled a soft folded fabric from it and opened it. "Listen. 'The arms are fair, when the intent of bearing them is just.'" Her great-aunt gasped. "Raymond is telling us to restore Belle Haven ourselves! To roll up our shirtsleeves, so to speak." She jumped up. "I must show this to Bertie."

When Cornelia reached the doorway, she turned around. "Oh, I almost forgot why I came looking for you. I just saw Albert poking around the old tobacco barn. We didn't hire him to restore that, did we?"

Jillian had no expectation of being able to get the cloth back, but at least Cornelia couldn't snatch the information it had given her. "No, that wasn't included in the estimate he gave us. He loves old buildings, so he's probably just looking it over on a break. I'll go make sure he's clear about it."

"Thank you, dear. Must run now." Cornelia disappeared from the room, her steps heading toward the stairs.

Jillian stood and headed downstairs to go out and find Albert. She didn't want him to think they didn't trust him, but since they weren't sure how they were going to pay for the three projects in the main house, she wanted to make sure he didn't get carried away looking for things they couldn't afford to have fixed.

By the time she picked her way through the overgrown back gardens to the tobacco barn, she saw no sign of the contractor. Perhaps he was back working on the windows. That was what Albert had planned to do all afternoon. Walking the perimeter of the plantation house, Jillian searched for signs of where Albert had last worked. Rounding a corner of the building, she was glad to see a ladder several feet in front of her. Relieved, she went to check how the repairs were looking.

When she got closer, the windows were still several feet

over her head and Jillian struggled to get a good look at Albert's workmanship. The ladder would help, so she walked around it to climb higher. Grasping the rungs at her shoulder height, Jillian looked down for the bottom step. That's when she noticed the boot prints. There was something about them. A cold realization spread through her, and she bent down for a closer look. They were exactly like the prints she'd seen near the body of Otis Dupree!

"It wasn't my fault. Now you're gonna wish you had never figured it out."

"**D**on't turn around!" Albert commanded.

"I know who you are, Albert. Why can't I turn around?" Jillian asked, stalling for the time to figure out a strategy. "What happened? Why did you murder Otis?"

"It wasn't murder! I told you it wasn't my fault."

Jillian inched to her right.

"Quit moving! I'm warning you."

Freezing, Jillian tried to read Albert's shadow moving along the wall of the house. When she saw the outline of a long-handled tool being raised, she waited as long as she dared, stepped between the ladder and the house, and heaved into it with all her strength, knocking it over and into the contractor's body. As the ladder fell, it dislodged the hoe from Albert's hand and knocked him to the ground. The impact yanked the ladder out of Jillian's hand, and she saw Albert still moving, crawling toward the farm tool.

Her feet felt cemented to the ground, but with one massive effort, she dove for the hoe as Albert reached his closest hand for it. Instead of grabbing it, her foot knocked it closer to her attacker. Albert picked up the tool and stood, towering over her. Jillian closed her eyes. *At least my loved ones will know where I'm buried.*

The crack of a gunshot split the afternoon air. Lifting her head and opening her eyes, Jillian saw Bertie approaching, her old hunting rifle in hand. She also saw Albert collapsed flat to the ground, making Jillian fear he'd been hit.

"You make the tiniest move, and I promise I won't shoot

over your head this time." Bertie signaled for Jillian to move behind her. "I've got him covered. Cornelia already called the sheriff's department."

"Your timing was perfect, Bertie." Jillian's ears rang from the gunshot, and the rest of her tingled in relief. "And your aim was pretty good too."

The window above them opened, and Cornelia's head appeared. "How dare you try to kill my great-niece when we allowed you into our home, hired you, and even cooked for you. You're not at all like your sister."

Albert deflated, dropping his forehead to the ground. "No, I'm not. She knows nothing about any of this."

"Why did you kill Otis?" Jillian asked. She heard Bertie draw in a sharp breath.

The man lifted his head off the ground. "Can I sit up? I promise not to try anything." Sorrow flooded his face. "I don't want to embarrass Josi any more than I already have."

"All right, but don't think I won't shoot if you change your mind." Bertie stepped back but held her aim steady on him.

Slowly, Albert pushed up to his knees and then sat back. "I wasn't trying to kill him. I only wanted him to acknowledge that Josi and I are a part of the Dupree family." Albert's fingers clenched at the grass underneath. "When I found him, he was on a ladder out in the orchard. I wanted to show him proof, but he didn't want to see it. He laughed at me, like Josi and I were worthless. He thought we were gold diggers, just trying to get part of the Dupree estate. He told me to get off his land." Albert shook his head. "Then he took a swing at me with that cane of his. I was so angry I shook the ladder, but only to frighten him." His voice lowered to a whisper. "I didn't expect him to fall." He looked up at Jillian. "I knew you had figured it out when you started examining my boot prints."

Cornelia crossed her arms on the windowsill. "Otis didn't have any siblings, except a sister who died as a child. How could you be related?"

Albert shook his head. "We're descendants of Frederick Dupree."

Jillian gasped. "Frederick? How? He never made it out of Moss Hollow."

Bertie and Cornelia gaped at her. "And how do you know anything about this?" Bertie asked, still keeping a firm, steady grip on the gun.

"From that journal Savannah and I found while we were working in the attic," Jillian answered. "I've been putting the pieces together ever since, but I sure don't see how you and Josi could be involved in an old family story from 150 years ago."

"So that's why you asked me about the Dupree family," said Bertie.

Jillian acknowledged that it was. "The journal indicated Frederick had a wife and child, but I didn't see anything about them in the Moss Hollow history book I read. I really don't know what happened to them after Frederick went missing. And I don't know exactly how Albert and Josi could be tied into this sordid family mess."

"I have proof!" Albert thundered.

"I'm not arguing with you, Albert," Jillian said calmly. "Tell us about it." She hoped to keep Albert occupied until the officers arrived.

"When our mother died a couple of years ago, Josi and I were going through her things, deciding what to keep and what to discard or sell. I found an old strongbox with documents and old letters. There was an old family Bible that had a birth record from 1861. It showed Frederick Dupree as being the father of a boy, Harris, born in Moss Hollow. It also recorded the death of Frederick's wife, Charlotte, in Chattanooga, Tennessee, but there was nothing about Frederick. Apparently, he died in the Civil War, and his body was never accounted for. My mother had made a family tree, showing how her father was a direct descendant of Harris and Frederick Dupree."

"Frederick's wife must have moved away from Moss Hollow when he didn't come home."

Albert looked confused. "First you said Frederick didn't leave Moss Hollow. Now you say he didn't come home? That doesn't make sense. But then again, I've never been able to figure out what happened to him."

"You don't know?" Jillian had thought Albert had been looking for Frederick's burial place when Cornelia saw him lurking around the tobacco barn.

The man's eyes narrowed. "Know what?"

Reassured by Bertie's steady grip on the hunting rifle, Jillian took a deep breath. "Jedediah Dupree, one of Frederick's brothers, was sweet on Bridgett Summerlin, a niece of Vernon Belle. Jedediah and his parents were Southern sympathizers while Frederick was drawn to the Union cause. The brothers got into a fight in Bridgett's presence right here on Belle Haven land." Jillian looked at Albert, knowing what the impact of her next words would be. "Frederick died in that fight, and Jedediah convinced Bridgett to help him bury his brother beneath a large live oak tree in the back acreage. I'm sorry to say that I've not been able to find his unmarked grave."

Cornelia yelped. "We've had a Union soldier buried here all this time?"

"I don't think he had joined up yet," said Jillian. "I doubt there were any Union military offices in Georgia. From what Bridgett wrote, Frederick was preparing to take his family north when Jedediah snapped."

Jillian noticed a shudder shake Albert's shoulders. "Something I share with Jedediah," he said. "Ever since my mother's death and then my stroke, it's like I have a second man inside me." He turned toward Jillian, his eyes glistening with tears. "I am so sorry."

The three women exchanged glances. Jillian hadn't heard of Albert's stroke. Could that have been a factor behind his uncontrolled anger?

The wail of a patrol car's siren drew closer, and Gooder and Laura Lee soon ran around the corner of the house. Gooder pulled his gun and trained it on Albert.

Jillian explained what had transpired to the two deputies.

"So Otis's death *wasn't* an accident," Laura Lee said to Gooder's obvious chagrin.

"Well, you should have trusted us to get to the bottom of it all, Jillian," Gooder said. "You can put your rifle away, Mrs. Harper," he said over his shoulder to Bertie. "We'll take it from here."

Bertie lowered her weapon but continued to cradle it in her arms while Laura Lee handcuffed Albert and led him away.

Cornelia yelled down to Gooder from her perch. "Young man, you owe Jillian an apology. She was right about those strange boot prints belonging to Otis's killer. See?" She reached so far out of the window to point out the prints that Jillian feared she was in danger of tumbling down.

"Oh, for heaven's sake, Cornelia," Bertie snapped at her sister. "Come out here before you hurt yourself."

"All right, but don't say anything interesting until I get there." Cornelia disappeared.

Gooder holstered his gun and kneeled to look at the prints. "So this little difference between these two prints told you this man was Otis's killer?" His eyes contained a fair amount of doubt.

Jillian nodded. "That on top of the fact that he tried to kill me with a hoe when he saw me examining them."

"And don't forget about Albert saying he hadn't *meant* to kill Otis," Cornelia added as she approached them.

Jillian nodded at her great-aunt's statement. "But Albert said something right before you arrived that might have a bearing on all this."

Gooder rose from his crouch. "What was that?"

The three women told the deputy about Albert's stroke.

"Of course, you'll want to verify that with his doctor and his sister, but we think it is an extenuating circumstance," said Cornelia. "I don't think we're going to be pressing charges. Right, girls?"

Bertie and Jillian nodded in agreement.

Gooder's face didn't reveal much, but Jillian guessed that if he didn't follow up, Laura Lee would, especially after a gentle nudge from her fellow Sweetie Pies. He made some notes. "Getting back to the prints. Do any of you ladies know why the one boot is different?"

The three ladies stared at him, silent. The deputy sheriff had moved to examine the ladder and hoe when Bertie spoke.

"I don't know for sure, but Albert is part of the Dupree family line, and Dupree men often had a hereditary trait of one leg being slightly shorter than the other. An insert to accommodate that might create a different look to the print. Otis was afflicted with it. That's why he walked with a cane."

Bertie's explanation made so much sense to Jillian and was something she hadn't known. She wondered if any of the three Dupree brothers—Frederick, Jedediah, or Elliot—had suffered from the handicap.

"We'll examine the boots and look into your suggestions," Gooder told her. "The techs will dust the hoe for prints and take some photos. But you ladies can go inside. We'll call you if we need anything else." He turned away from them to resume his work.

Jillian linked her arms with Bertie and Cornelia. "I don't know about you two, but I'm starving."

"I ate the rest of the quiche earlier, but Bertie and I will whip up something," said Cornelia.

Jillian gave her great-aunt's arm a squeeze, thankful for such a normal activity after such an extraordinary afternoon.

Within an hour, the three women were gathered at the table with a simple meal of black-eyed peas and corn bread. As she ate, Jillian's mind continued to process everything she'd learned.

"Aunt Cornelia, do you have that piece of cloth you took from me upstairs?"

"Oh, you mean the message from Raymond?"

"No, I mean the message from Bridgett. Or at least I'm pretty sure it is."

"I still have it in my pocket," Cornelia said. "I was on my way to show it to Bertie when everything happened with that nasty contractor." She retrieved it, handing it to Jillian.

The cloth indeed was adorned with the quote from Shakespeare's *Henry IV*. Below the words was finely embroidered: *In memory of Frederick Dupree,* and it was signed in thread: *Bridgett Summerlin, 1861.* Jillian sat back as the last pieces of the puzzle floated into place.

"What is it, Jillian?" Bertie asked, concerned about her silence.

"Nothing is wrong," Jillian said. "I just figured out the last of this mystery." She showed her grandmother the quote, explaining the significance and the connection with Union sympathizers. "I don't know if Bridgett became a secret Yankee or not, but she was jarred by the small civil war she had witnessed in the Dupree family. There is no indication that she and Jedediah continued their courtship, so I assume that she broke it off while honoring her promise not to tell the Duprees what had happened."

"So they never married?" Cornelia interjected.

"I don't think so. I think Bridgett returned to her mountains of Tennessee and the rest of her immediate family. But I think she left her prized journal and this embroidered piece as bread crumbs to lead someone, someday, to the truth of what happened to Frederick. I doubt that we will ever find his grave. We would have to dig around every live oak in the back acreage, and we still might not find him. Up to today, I had thought that we should try so he could be buried with his family in the Dupree crypt in town." She drew in a deep breath. "Some mysteries are never meant to be solved. I think we should just let Frederick rest in peace."

"That makes sense, dear," Cornelia said.

"One thing does seem odd to me, though," Jillian said. "Otis was so well off, but he never put lifts in his shoe. Surely it would have been more comfortable."

A strangled noise came from her grandmother.

Jillian looked over to see a tear skimming down her cheek. "Bertie, what's wrong?"

The older woman's face crumpled. "It was all my fault." Her voice wobbled, and she shook her head, covering her face with her napkin.

Cornelia covered Bertie's free hand gently. "Do you want me to tell her?"

Her grandmother nodded, dropping the napkin long enough to add, "No embellishment, Sister."

"I promise," said Cornelia. "Jillian, I'm sure it's no surprise to you that your grandmother has always had the sharp wit we all know and love. But when she was a young girl, she was what today might be called a mean girl. Otis was one of her favorite targets. She teased him for the limp he had because of the shorter leg. Other kids joined in, and Otis took it really hard. To compensate, he grew hard-hearted and meaner than Bertie ever was. He refused any special shoes or medical procedures. That cane of his became his constant companion."

Bertie turned her head away and stared out the window.

"Otis's transformation woke Bertie up to the harm words can do. She began to change too, but in the opposite direction."

"Today, I would have been called a bully," Bertie said, breaking in. "I tried to apologize, but it was too late and it backfired. Otis thanked me for helping him 'embrace the person I truly am.' Those were his words."

"She's never forgiven herself, Jillian," Cornelia added. "Sister, it's time. Long past time."

Jillian realized her grandmother's spell at the funeral home had not been a physical collapse but an emotional one. Guilt carried over so many decades had been a crushing weight. "Bertie, you turned from your old ways and tried to make amends. You're not responsible for how Otis chose to respond. He chose bitter, while you chose better. You were just a kid. You really need to let it go. And believe me, I know that's much easier said than done."

Bertie dabbed at the corners of her eyes with the napkin. "I have a lot to think about, but your words help. Thank you." She climbed to her feet and left the room.

Through the years Jillian had always thought of Bertie as the unchangeable one among them. Now she realized her grandmother had perhaps changed more than anyone she knew.

By the following Sunday, things were somewhat back to normal, and the Southern Sweetie Pies gathered at the bakery for their regular meeting.

"Bertie was worried those two days without power would kill the week's income," Cornelia told the group. "It turns out that one of us almost being hoed to death is wonderful for sales."

"And so is being rescued by your gun-totin' grandmother," Jillian added. "Bertie's almost famous. For the next fifteen minutes, anyway."

Her grandmother crossed her arms. "I could do without the gawking, but I'm thankful for the increase in business."

Annalise stirred some sugar into her coffee. "I heard that Albert will be charged only with voluntary manslaughter."

"That's right," Laura Lee said. "His attorney is working on a plea bargain that will take into account his medical history and his clean record. He will probably be sentenced to a short jail term and several years' probation. He'll get the counseling he needs too."

Glancing at the wall clock, Savannah sighed. "I was hoping Josi would still feel welcome and come this afternoon, but I guess it was too much for her. I understand, but I really don't think she had any idea what Albert had done."

Laura Lee nodded. "At work I've learned how to stay as neutral and calm as possible, but when we had to question Josi . . . Well, that was tough. I felt horrible for her, and Albert was almost beside himself about what all this would do to his sister."

"Josi must be feeling mighty alone," said Lenora, who had returned to her apartment over the shop. "Even the women at the Clip & Curl think Josi's innocent of any wrongdoing, but they don't know how to help the girl."

Annalise set her coffee cup on the counter. "That's it. I'm going over to Josi's house to see if I can convince her to come back here with me."

"That's a great idea," Jillian told her. "I'll start on the Idiot's Delight Cake, and maybe we can give it to Josi to take home with her, if she comes." After the successful baking attempt at the prior meeting, Jillian was ready to take another crack at the recipe that had previously been such a disaster. "So come to the kitchen when you get back."

Annalise left, and the six other women returned to the kitchen. "What do you need to do first, Jillian?" Lenora asked as they surrounded the work space.

"I already set the oven to preheat," Jillian told her. "And I'm using a thermometer to make sure the oven is the right temperature."

The women nodded their approval. "And I rewrote the recipe because the original one I used didn't order the steps right, so I was scrambling to finish the batter before the sauce on the stove was ruined. I'll start with the batter this time."

Cornelia clapped her hands. "You're learning how to make a recipe work for you and adapting. *Brava!*"

"That's an important point," Laura Lee said. "When I started making changes to recipes, instead of slavishly following one even if it wasn't working out for me, my baking jumped to a whole new level."

"Well, don't stand there talking about it," Bertie said gruffly, even though her eyes were encouraging. "Start mixing the batter."

Jillian saluted her grandmother. "Aye, aye, Captain." All the eyes trained on her every movement would have rendered her frozen a few months ago, but Jillian knew they were there to help, not to nitpick. With a smile, she began combining the batter ingredients.

She had placed the pan of Idiot's Delight batter into the oven and was closing the door when the bell on the shop's front door sounded. Collectively, the six women held their breaths. When Annalise came through to the kitchen with Josi behind her, Jillian wanted to let out a whoop. She held off because she didn't want to scare her off.

"Josi, we're so glad you've come," Cornelia said. "Jillian has just put the Idiot's Delight cake into the oven and set the timer. Would you like some coffee?"

Josi looked like she was about to cry.

"Or tea, dear. Your choice," Cornelia hastened to add.

"All of you are so kind." Josi's voice wobbled. "I don't know how to thank you."

Laura Lee grinned at their anxious friend. "Now that you mention it, I've been waiting for ages in the queue to check out the new Robert Galbraith book. If you could bump me forward a bit, I'd sure appreciate it. Thanks."

"I can hear it at the Clip & Curl now," said Savannah. "'Did you hear that Deputy Zane is taking favors from the Moss Hollow library? Must be a bribe, don'tcha think?'"

The ladies all laughed, including Josi.

When the chuckles subsided, Josi spoke up. "I don't think that would look very good on my résumé. But between you and me, some librarians do it regularly."

"Why should your résumé matter?" asked Cornelia. "You have a perfectly good job already."

Josi lowered her eyes. "Well, I don't know if the town will want me to stay, now that Albert's—"

"Nonsense," Bertie blurted, then dialed back on her tone. "I mean, why would people judge you for your brother going through what's probably a medical issue that caused his behavior? Sure, there will be gossip, but folks know you weren't involved."

"And that's from someone who would have the most reason to judge," Savannah pointed out.

Jillian looked Josi in the eyes and smiled. "I know a little something about being regarded suspiciously and gossiped about too, but if you stick around long enough, the folks of Moss Hollow will eventually come around. They'll see you for who you really are."

The little town had worked its way back into Jillian's heart, she realized. It was home, and she hoped Josi would experience that feeling too.

Josi drew in a shaky breath. "Do you really think so?" The women around her all nodded. "Then I'll give it a try."

The atmosphere in the shop became lighter, and the women turned to other subjects, like who Otis had named to inherit the Dupree estate.

"Well, I know it won't be Albert and me," Josi said. "I didn't know anything about our connection with the Dupree family until Albert filled me in after his . . . well, his arrest. I guess we could have retained a lawyer and litigated the whole thing, but neither of us thought that would be the right thing to do. Mr. Dupree's lawyer sought us out. I think he was a bit nervous about the whole matter. But both of us signed a waiver saying we would not seek any part of the estate. All Albert ever wanted was to be accepted by the rest of the family."

Savannah winked at Jillian. "I heard from Harold Johnson that Otis left him the lion's share of the land, including the peach orchard, of course. He also said the mansion was going to Dorothy Haines."

The women gaped at their friend. "Otis Dupree left his estate to his hired help?" Laura Lee laughed. "I sure didn't see that coming."

Jillian found herself grinning from the inside out. She had never expected to agree with anything Otis did, but she applauded this one. Once the buzz had dissipated, Jillian drew Bridgett's journal from her bag. "I found something that I want you all to hear. Every time I read this, I seem to find something interesting."

The women quieted down to listen as Jillian read:

September 1861: I attended a meeting of a new group in town with Aunt Olive today. The women meet to bake together, share recipes, and roll bandages for the soldiers. They call themselves the Southern Sweetie Pies, and they are the most gracious ladies I've met in Georgia.

Jillian looked up at the surprised exclamations. "Did you all know the Sweetie Pies have been around so long?"

"I always thought Bertie and Cornelia started it," Savannah confessed.

Cornelia laughed. "Not by a long shot. I like to think of the Southern Sweetie Pies as a living, breathing historical monument."

"They truly are," Jillian said. She ran a hand over the leather cover of the journal. "I'd love to know more about what happened to Bridgett after she left Moss Hollow."

"Do you know for sure she went back to Tennessee?" Savannah asked.

"Well, Bridgett wrote about how her father was arriving the next day to take her home in the last entry, so I assume so," said Jillian.

Annalise opened her purse. "I found something that will help." She removed a clear plastic bag and handed it to Jillian. "It was in a keepsake album owned by Mary Stansel."

Inside the plastic was a very old photo postcard of a woman, man, and two little girls. Jillian turned the photo over and gasped.

"Don't just stand there gawking. What does it say?" Lenora asked.

Jillian cleared her throat and read:

August 5, 1873

Dearest Mary,

William finally took us to the ocean. Saida and Lizzy absolutely loved it in Cape May, New Jersey, and so did I. Nothing will ever take the place of our Tennessee mountains, but the beach life is wonderful for a short change.

Greetings to all,

Bridgett Yancey

Cornelia clapped her hands. "Hooray! Poor Bridgett fell first for a murderer, but then she went on to find a nice husband who took her on vacations. See? There's hope for you too."

The timer Jillian had set cut in over the laughter. "The moment of truth," she muttered, drawing on a pair of oven mitts. She removed the pan from the oven and carried it over to the counter. Everyone gathered around, peering down.

Jillian watched her grandmother.

Bertie looked up from the cake. "You did it, Jillian. It looks like a real Idiot's Delight cake."

She laughed. "Now it only has to taste like a real Idiot's Delight cake, but we'll have to wait for it to cool."

When the Sweetie Pies sampled the cake, they all agreed it tasted like the real thing.

"You can stop wondering if you'll make a real baker, dear," said Cornelia. "You already are."

Guilty Confections
Book Two Recipe

Here is the simple recipe for an Idiot's Delight Cake baked by Jillian Green and approved by the Southern Sweetie Pies.

Idiot's Delight Cake
Batter

7 tablespoons butter, softened
½ cup sugar
1 cup flour

2 teaspoons baking powder
½ cup milk

Sauce

4 cups water
1 tablespoon butter
1 cup brown sugar
1 cup raisins

1 teaspoon vanilla

Instructions

Preheat oven to 375 degrees.

1. To make the batter, cream the butter and sugar together.

2. Sift the flour and baking powder together.

3. Add flour mixture to the creamed mixture, alternating with the milk; set aside.

4. To make the sauce, combine the water, butter, brown sugar, and raisins in a saucepan and bring to a light boil.

5. Meanwhile, drop spoonfuls of the batter into a greased 9 x 13-inch baking pan.

6. Stir the vanilla into the sauce and pour the sauce over the batter.

7. Bake for 25 to 30 minutes.

Learn more about Annie's fiction books at

AnniesFiction.com

- Access your e-books
- Discover exciting new series
- Read sample chapters
- Watch video book trailers
- Share your feedback

We've designed the Annie's Fiction website especially for you!

Plus, manage your account online!

- Check your account status
- Make payments online
- Update your address

 ANNIE'S ATTIC MYSTERIES®

 CREATIVE WOMAN MYSTERIES®

 Annie's Quilted Mysteries™

 Annie's Mysteries Unraveled™

 AMISH INN MYSTERIES™

 ANNIE'S SECRETS of the QUILT™

 Chocolate Shoppe Mysteries™

 SECRETS OF THE CASTLETON MANOR LIBRARY™

Visit us at AnniesFiction.com